A small, round vial fell lightly into his palm.

"The Devil water," Cucho said without breathing.

Sacrette held the vial carefully to the thin light beaming into the cave.

"What is it, Thunder?" asked Farnsworth.

Taking a deep breath, Sacrette exhaled slowly. "It appears to be some kind of chemical liquid. Very heavy in nature."

"What kind of liquid?" Farnsworth tried to lean toward Sacrette.

Sacrette felt a chill streak along his spine. "From what Cucho has described...the type used in biological warfare."

———————————————

Also by Tom Willard

Strikefighters

Published by
HARPER PAPERBACKS

STRIKE FIGHTERS

BOLD FORAGER

TOM WILLARD

Harper Paperbacks

Harper & Row, Publishers, New York
Grand Rapids, Philadelphia, St. Louis, San Francisco
London, Singapore, Sydney, Tokyo, Toronto

This is a work of fiction. The characters, incidents, and
dialogues are products of the author's imagination and are not
to be construed as real. Any resemblance to actual events or
persons, living or dead, is entirely coincidental.

Harper Paperbacks a division of Harper & Row, Publishers, Inc.
10 East 53rd Street, New York, N.Y. 10022

Cover art by Attila Hejja

First printing: October, 1990

Printed in the United States of America

HARPER PAPERBACKS and colophon are trademarks of
Harper & Row, Publishers, Inc.

10 9 8 7 6 5 4 3 2 1

For my nephew Daniel John LeDuc.
My lovely, oval-eyed niece Emma Nicole Lipp.
And...
Especially for Modesto Del Busto, who survived the tyranny of Fidel Castro's persecution, and came to the United States to teach American college students the essence of dignity, courage, freedom, and the sacredness of liberty.

Cuba Libre!

BOLD FORAGER

Prologue

Punta del Soldato Francés. Cuba.

FRENCH SOLDIER'S POINT JUTTED SOUTHWARD FROM the white sandy beach, its verdant foliage a deep green, except in the treetops, where thousands of the Point's namesakes—the French soldier finch—painted a myriad of moving colors with their ruffling red breasts, flapping green wings, and darting blue heads.

On the long stretch of beach below, a sign painted in bold red letters warned:

RESTRICTED AREA. VIOLATORS WILL BE
PROSECUTED!

Ignoring the sign, three young boys played baseball in the sand surrounding a small cove as they did every afternoon since they could remember. There was no reason for them to notice the sign, or the finches, with any particular interest. They had seen the sign and birds since childhood, and figured they would see both until their deaths in old age.

Such were the expectations for all the people of their obscure fishing village nestled along the southwest coast of Cuba.

Cucho Clemente, a black-eyed, brown sugar-skinned boy of thirteen, stood near the tree line balancing a homemade bat on his shoulder. Closer to scrawny than skinny, he had thin arms and a flat chest that belied the strength of his powerful wrists; strength built from the rigors of working a fishing boat and swinging the bat daily. He wore a dirty T-shirt; scrawled on the back of the shirt, in charcoal, was the name CANSECO.

His hero. The powerful home run hitter of the Oakland A's was Cuban, and though considered a political outcast, the rich and famous American baseball player was openly idolized by thousands of Cuban youngsters. More even than Che Guevara, or Fidel Castro himself.

The idolatry was known by the government, who accepted the fact that great men of destiny stood several rungs beneath the gods of the Palaestra. Especially in the eyes of children, whose loyalties would change as they matured into adults. And become good Fidelistos.

In place of a real baseball, the boys used small coconuts still in their pulpy green shells. Real baseballs were nonexistent in the village. Coconuts grew in abundance, and if lost in the surf, were no real loss.

"Texas leaguer," Cucho shouted. He tossed the coconut into the air; the bat snapped at the falling target, making contact. A sharp crack rang across the cove.

In the shallow water offshore, the two boys broke the serenity of the surface as they scurried toward the incoming pop fly.

A thudding sound followed as Alessandro Diaz caught the fly ball between his bare hands. Automatically the muscular boy threw the coconut back to Cucho.

"Line drive," Cucho shouted to Juan, Alessandro's brother, the shortest of the trio. Momentarily the coconut flew from the bat in a straight line.

Juan made the catch inches above the water, reeled toward the beach, then rifled the makeshift ball to Cucho.

Over and over Cucho would hit the ball to the Diaz brothers, who had become his brothers over the nearly five years since the death of his parents in a hurricane.

An hour later the boys lay in the sand, staring at the sky that seemed to stretch endlessly to the south.

"Jose Canseco has been sent to the minor leagues," Cucho said nonchalantly while biting into a papaya.

"I didn't know he was in the minor leagues. I thought he was in the majors," Alessandro spoke with genuine surprise.

"He went to the minors after he injured his hand," Cucho replied, shaking his head.

"Where did they send him?" Alessandro asked.

Cucho shrugged. He wasn't certain. "Somewhere in North America. Probably Miami."

"Why did they send him to the minors?" Juan asked. "My hands always hurt and I can still play."

Cucho laughed. "You're not a major leaguer, Juan. To be a major leaguer means you have to be perfect. But he'll soon be back."

"Back where? In Cuba?" Alessandro's voice sounded excited.

"*Estúpido!*" Cucho teased. "Back in the majors."

A long silence followed. Suddenly Juan bolted upright. There was a curious look on his face. "How do you know this, Cucho?"

A broad grin crawled across Cucho's face. "I heard it on the radio. Voice of America."

Alessandro looked worried as he slowly stood up beside Cucho. He thought for a moment. There was only one way he could have heard a broadcast of an American baseball game over the Spanish-language Voice of America.

There were no radios in their village of Santa Rosa, except the shortwave radios on the fishing boats, all of which were on a low-frequency, government-controlled maritime band.

In a voice that was no more than a whisper, Alessandro said what they all knew to be the truth. "You have been to La Casa del Diablo!"

The mere thought of the secret military facility ten miles east of French Soldier's Point sent a chill through Alessandro. La Casa del Diablo—the House of the Devil, as it was known to locals—was a place where many entered, and from where few returned.

"You must have been insane." Juan was shaking his head as he spoke.

Cucho shrugged. "I've been there many times."

Momentary fear was quickly replaced by exhilaration.

"Tell us," Juan pleaded.

"Please," begged Alessandro.

The brothers were squatting like coiled reptiles, giving Cucho the feeling that they might spring into outer space if their questions weren't answered.

Cucho sat back in lordly fashion; when certain that he had their full attention, he revealed the source of his secret knowledge.

He pointed to the terrain beyond where the warning sign stood, marking the beginning of the restricted zone. "Casa del Diablo is surrounded by a tall fence with sharp barbed wire at the top. Soldiers with guns and vicious dogs patrol the grounds. It is a very dangerous place."

"How did you get inside the fence?" asked Alessandro.

"Like a ghost," Cucho replied. "I walked through a hole in the fence."

"You are insane," Juan said breathlessly.

Alessandro looked at him suspiciously. "I have heard there are land bombs planted in the ground along the edge of the fence. How could you walk through there and not get killed?"

"The first night, I stayed outside of the fence." Cucho laughed. "The second night, I saw a man appear from the jungle near the fence. A tall man. Not one like us. A fair-skinned man with yellow hair."

"One of the Europeans I have heard my father mention," Alessandro interrupted.

Cucho nodded. "The European was carrying a piece of paper. He seemed to be following directions from the paper."

"Perhaps it was a map through the land bombs," said Alessandro.

"Yes. A map. He walked across the ground where the land bombs were planted, and went to the fence."

"What did he do?" asked Juan.

Cucho shrugged. "He cut a small hole in the fence, then disappeared into the jungle."

"You went through the hole?" Juan asked incredulously.

Cucho nodded. "His feet left prints for me to follow. I stepped in each of his footprints."

The brothers shook their heads in sheer disbelief. "What did you do next?" asked Alessandro.

"I followed the footprints to a trail. I walked along the trail until I came to small buildings that looked like they were set into the ground. They were made of concrete. Guards and dogs were everywhere. That's when I heard the American baseball game."

"How?" blurted Juan, whose fascination with Cucho's journey into Casa del Diablo had made him completely forget the baseball game.

"The radio was playing from speakers mounted on tall poles. I guess they let the soldiers listen to the baseball game. Perhaps to keep them from falling asleep on guard."

"That's when you heard about Canesco?" Alessandro was nodding his head knowingly.

"It was the All-Star game. The announcer said Canesco was the first baseball player in the minors to be voted into an All-Star game."

"Did he play?" The question came from Alessandro.

"No," Cucho replied. "He was in the minors. Only majors can play."

The brothers looked at Cucho admiringly.

Alessandro started to speak when suddenly the air was shattered by a long wave of stammering gunfire from the trees above French Soldier's Point.

All eyes turned instinctively as the pulsating throb of helicopter rotors beat the air.

"Look!" Juan was pointing at a camouflaged object hovering over the Point.

The markings were clear on the Hind Mil-24 Soviet-built gunship. Bearing the markings of the Fuerza Aerea Revolucionara, a white star set in a red triangle superimposed onto a blue circle, the Cuban air force gunship gave no doubt of its intent as it dove toward the trees.

"Run!" shouted Juan, moving like the devil was in

pursuit. Close behind, Cucho and Alessandro followed the frightened boy into the tree line.

The gunship circled over French Soldier's Point, then turned on a long downwind gun-run, leaving no doubt of its purpose when a tongue of machine-gun fire streaked from the four 20mm cannons mounted in the nose turrets.

The tree line exploded under the devastating force of the vicious storm of bullets. Branches, stripped from their trunks, shot skyward like matchsticks; coconuts ruptured like eggs dropped from a tall building.

Suddenly the sky came alive as thousands of French soldier finches dissolved instantly, momentarily filling the air with red, green, and blue feathers that disappeared as another storm of cannon fire from the Mil-24 shook the tree line.

"*Madre Mia,*" Cucho whispered.

"They know you were on Casa del Diablo!" Juan cried to Cucho. "They have come for you, Cucho!"

Cucho said nothing in reply. Instead, he was watching the Point where the bullets were devastating the trees as the helicopter made another assault.

The pilot flew an easterly heading, and it was apparent to the boys that he was firing at something in the jungle. Something the pilot knew was there, but couldn't see.

Seconds later the sky shook as the helicopter thundered over the Point and disappeared beyond their line of vision.

It was in that instant, while the helicopter was rotating for another pass at French Soldier's Point, that a flash of golden movement within the green of the jungle caught Cucho's eye.

"Look!" Cucho was pointing at the jungle where a rocky outcropping jutted out toward the cove.

A man was standing on the rocks. A man with golden hair.

"It's him!" Cucho said softly. "The man from the fence."

As though he had heard Cucho, the man turned toward where the boys lay hidden.

Instinctively, the boys pulled deeper into the jungle.

"What's he doing?" Juan asked no one in particular.

"He's going to be killed," said Alessandro.

"Look." Cucho pointed at the golden-haired man.

As the sky began to shudder with the approach of the helicopter, the man glanced around, then reached inside his shirt. His hand reappeared, clutching a small, shiny ball-like object.

The man's arm flashed outward, toward the cove. The shiny globe arced against the blue sky. The boys' eyes followed the flight path of the object until it struck the water in the cove and disappeared.

Without looking back, the man began threading his way down the hill. At the precise moment he reached the beach, the helicopter appeared over the Point.

Spotting the man, the Hind darted from the sky in low, predatorlike pursuit.

Another stream of bullets flashed from the gunship's nose turret. Tearing at the sand, the deadly projectiles stitched a trail of large holes that chased the running man's footsteps.

Lying in the undergrowth, the boys saw the man's face as the bullets ripped through his back and exploded from his chest, turning the white shirt he was wearing into a blood-soaked dark crimson.

So great was the impact, the man was lifted onto his toes, where he seemed to hang above the beach as his body was carried forward by the force of the bullets.

He fell in a heap less than ten meters from where the boys watched the deadly scenario unfold, and they could see that he was still alive.

His hands twitched as the roar of the Hind became a steady drone in an approach to landing on the beach. Sensing something nearby, the man found the strength to raise his head slightly.

In the tree line, hidden from view, Cucho leaned through the heavy brush to find the man staring at him.

Their eyes joined momentarily. Cucho thought he saw the man's head motion to the side, as though signaling him away.

Seconds later an officer in the Cuban army approached with a drawn pistol.

It was then that Cucho understood.

The dying man pulled a hand grenade from beneath his bloodstained shirt. Feverishly he pulled at the pin with his teeth as the officer shouted.

In that split second before death would claim him, the man appeared to grow calm. Cucho thought he saw a smile, as though the man had won something more important than his life.

The spoon kicked from the hand grenade!

The officer fell back, running for the safety of the helicopter.

A deep, dull explosion rocked the beach, spewing sand and human flesh in a mushrooming cloud that turned gray, then red, finally a deep charcoal black.

Seconds later the air returned to its pristine blue.

More helicopters appeared, emptying from their bellies several dozen camouflage-clad soldiers who quickly sealed off the beach.

"Come," Cucho whispered to the brothers. "We must leave."

Moving quietly, like shadows through the thick underbrush, the boys melted into the jungle, taking with them the images of what they had seen.

The man with golden hair. The roar of the helicopter gunship. The spitting death of the cannons.

But more importantly, to Cucho, the memory of the globe arcing toward the cove.

A globe that reminded him of a shiny, precious baseball!

PART ONE: ▮▮▮▮▮▮ LA CASA DEL DIABLO

2100.

FROM THIRTY THOUSAND FEET THE BLACKNESS OF night blanketed the leading edge of hurricane Hugo. Through his night-vision goggles, Commander Boulton Sacrette could see the storm's gyrating mass stretching from the West Indies to the Dominican Republic. With its eye over Puerto Rico, the next stop on Hugo's agenda would be Haiti, then Cuba, which lay beneath Sacrette's twelve o'clock nose position.

"Home Plate . . . Wolf One at Angels thirty-two. Passing over Cuba."

From somewhere south of Jamaica, the voice of a naval radio operator on the nuclear aircraft carrier USS *Valiant* replied, "Roger, Wolf One. Have you on the scope. Turn to heading two-zero-zero. Maintain Angels thirty-two. We don't want Fidel's boys to get nervous."

Looking down, Sacrette could see the lights of Havana burning blue-green beneath his right wing. "No problem. Have Havana in sight beneath starboard wing. Camaguey coming under left wing. We'll stay up here in the 'safe zone' until we're out of their territory."

Turning onto the new heading, Sacrette glanced around the cockpit, then to the sky. The moon appeared blue through the goggles, and he smiled. The smile was obscured by the strange-looking "Cat's Eye" prism night-vision goggles covering his face.

"Sing us a couple of lines from 'Blue Moon,' Chief." Sacrette was speaking to the man riding in the "pit," the rear seat of the sleek jetfighter.

"To hell with 'Blue Moon'! CPO Desmond "Diamonds" Farnsworth responded gruffly. "I'll be glad to get back to the carrier. Flying along the edge of a hurricane isn't my idea of how to spend a fun-filled evening."

"No sweat, Diamonds. We'll stay out here on the edge. A few bumps and thermals. Nothing to worry about. I'll have you tucked in and sipping Johnny Walker Red aboard the carrier in thirty minutes."

Looking out the cockpit through the image-intensifier tubes of his "Cat's Eye" goggles, Farnsworth scowled at Cuba, which was swimming in a sea of soft blue-green light.

"This is weird, Thunderbolt," Farnsworth said, using Sacrette's running name. "Everything looks blue. Or green. I'm not sure which. But it's damned weird." Farnsworth wore a similar NVG unit.

"We're night attack-configured now, Chief. For the first time. No more relying on good weather in order to use STARLIGHT. No more ground or airborne illumination. No more slewing the FLIR. I can see outside the cockpit as though the sun was shining straight from above."

"Yeah. Like a couple of hoot owls."

Sacrette chuckled at the black crew chief's apt description. "Which reminds me. What time frame are we looking at to get the entire twenty-four Hornets in the wing night-equipped?"

Farnsworth thought for a moment. "The technicians at China Lake told us the system could be installed in a matter of hours. All we need is the equipment. More importantly, how long before your jet jocks will be checked out?"

"About the same. Mostly familiarization."

"Familiarization? Discomfort indoctrination is more like it. I don't see how you can fly wearing all this on your face."

Sacrette laughed. "It's like sitting in an optometrist's chair looking through one of those machines used to examine eyes. You get used to the goggles. While you were learning how to install and pull maintenance on the unit, I was learning how to put it to use. We'll have the wing seeing in the dark by the end of the month."

"Yeah. Instead of calling us the VFA-101 Fighting Hornets, we'll be the Fighting Hoot Owls."

As he glanced at the sleek needle-nose protruding beyond the cockpit, Sacrette felt his chest swell with pride. He was the CAG, the commander of the air wing group of the nuclear aircraft carrier USS *Valiant*. His was the first uniformly designed strike/attack wing in the US Navy to base both light and heavy strike missions and fighter attack missions around a single aircraft. Sacrette flew the McDonnell Douglas F/A-18 Hornet: the world's newest supersonic **Strike/Fighter!**

"The F-18 is a magnificent aircraft, Chief. The Navy knew what it was doing when the Hornet was selected for carrier duty. My job has certainly been simplified. Instead of being the CAG of three squadrons to carry out strike and fighter duty, there's just the one F-18 Strike/Fighter squadron, and the one F-14 Tomcat squadron for long-range fighter missions. No more A-6s or A-7s for strike missions. The *Valiant*'s air wing is more diversified by the operation of a single aircraft that can do the job of several other types. What a machine."

Farnsworth couldn't find an argument with the CAG. "The Hornet certainly saves money for the taxpayers by rolling all the combat missions into one design. Not to mention maintenance. Yes, sir. She's a great aircraft."

Sacrette started to speak, but was stopped by a slight yaw of the nose.

A split second later a chill raced along his spine. And then he heard what he instinctively knew would follow.

A loud buzzer filled the cockpit. An eerie red glow pierced the blue-green glow filling the cockpit.

"We've got a fire light, Thunderbolt!" Diamonds shouted excitedly.

As he glanced quickly at the engine monitor indicator on the left side of the instrument panel, Sacrette's blue eyes widened at the oil pressure gauge framed within the EMI.

"Oil pressure's sinking toward bottom. Extinguisher activated." His hands moved quickly across the instrument panel to the fire extinguisher button.

"Shutting down port engine." Moving gracefully, without panic, Sacrette's fingers began shutting down the left engine.

"Going to single engine power. Contact the *Valiant*, Chief. I've got my hands full," Sacrette ordered.

"Roger," Farnsworth replied. Quickly he tuned in the emergency frequency and issued their signal. "Home Plate, this is Wolf One. Have lost port engine. Repeat. Have lost port engine."

From the *Valiant*'s combat information center, the radioman responded after a short pause. "Roger, Wolf One. Understand you are declaring emergency. Stand by for instructions."

Looking quickly to the pressure gauge of the starboard engine, he saw the falling needle make his only decision.

"Instructions, my ass. Son, I'm losing pressure in the starboard burner." Without another word, he changed frequency, skipping to the crypto channel that would keep his conversation segregated from satellite or ground-based Cuban radio monitors.

"Guantánamo ground approach. This is Wolf One, declaring single-engine failure. Losing pressure in other engine. Turn on the front lights, I'm coming your way."

Before the controller at the American naval base on the southeastern tip of Cuba could reply, Sacrette had pushed the nose over, applied left aileron, and kicked the rudder.

"Keep your eye on the radar screen, Chief. We might get company."

Two minutes later the cockpit shuddered under Farnsworth's warning report. Two bright blips burned on the green field of the rear seat APG-65 radar weapons system screen.

"We got bogies coming off the deck."

"Give me distance, bearing, and heading!" Thunderbolt ordered.

"Distance four–five miles... bearing zero-eight-zero on a heading of two-five-zero. Damn. They sure as hell aren't sight-seeing. They're closing for an intercept."

"Shut down the radar, then get ready, Chief. You

know how to operate the weapons system. Don't turn on the radar until absolutely necessary. We'll stay passive. Maybe they won't pick us up in the black hole of Calcutta."

Farnsworth switched off the radar. Flying without radar emitters would make the hunt more difficult for the Cuban pilots who no doubt would be tracking with their radar to find the fighter in the dark.

"System down, Thunderman. We can see them with the hoot owl eyes. But they won't be able to see us until we're right on top of them."

"Changes your mind about the goggles, doesn't it, Chief?"

"Barely," Farnsworth grumped approvingly from the pit.

Sacrette was scanning the sky below; passing through Angels twenty, he thought he saw something moving toward him along the Cuban coast.

Two dots, barely perceptible, began growing in size in his blue-green field of vision. Pointing toward the fighter planes, Sacrette sounded the alarm. "Tally ho!"

Farnsworth looked quickly. He could see the fighters, but couldn't determine their type. "What's the make and model?"

Sacrette squinted, then gripped both hands around the HOTAS, the hands-on-throttle-and-systems control stick between his legs. The HOTAS controlled everything from flight systems to communications, power and weapons systems. It was known as a "dream stick" by some pilots.

Farnsworth heard Sacrette laugh. "I don't believe my eyes."

"What is it, Thunderman. I can't make out diddlyshit through this crazy contraption."

"MiG-17 Frescos." His voice sounded more relaxed than moments before.

"You've got to be kidding," Farnsworth replied, dumbfounded.

"No, sir. I guess they don't know what we are, otherwise they'd at least send a 'Fishbed,' or 'Foxbat.'"

"The Fresco is a dinosaur. I didn't think they were still in service."

"Mostly third world Soviet-bloc allies. Like Cuba."

Noting that the swept wing fighters of Korean War vintage were closing the distance, Sacrette knew he had to make a decision.

"Hit the switch, Chief. Let's lock and load. They'll see us, but if we're not star-crossed, and other engine holds, we'll slip past them."

"Roger. Switch on." Farnsworth switched on the APG-65 radar weapons system.

"Screens up, Mr. Scott?" asked Sacrette, mimicking his favorite character from *Star Trek*.

"Aye, Captain. Up and pulsating. I got both of them square in my sights." Farnsworth was watching the screen. The two blips were flying in wing formation.

"Going to FLIR imaging, Chief." He glanced to the HUD mounted atop the instrument panel. The heads-up display projected vital aircraft information onto a transparent screen—information the pilot would ordinarily have to look for on the instrument panel. As the forward-looking infrared radar "cued" the Frescos through their heat sensors, Sacrette issued another order.

"Lock them up, Chief. Multiple targeting."

Calmly Farnsworth locked on to the Frescos' heat emission. Both fighters were now joined to the Strike/

Fighter by an invisible laser beam.

"Locked up."

On the HOTAS, Sacrette switched to the weapons system. Quickly he glanced to the port wingtip, where an AIM 9L heat-seeking Sidewinder missile waited for launch.

"You get one more chance, partner," Sacrette said softly to the images of the fighters.

"They've picked up our radar. They're on our ass!" Farnsworth called from the pit.

"Sorry 'bout that, Cubes." Sacrette pressed the firing switch.

"Fox Two," Farnsworth shouted, the signaling code that a Sidewinder had been fired.

"Fox Two," he repeated as Sacrette launched the second missile.

Two fiery tails streaked from the Hornet, reaching Mach 2.5 in a matter of seconds.

"Incoming!" Sacrette shouted as he saw the Frescos go missile-for-missile. Beyond the comet tails of the Sidewinders, a long tongue of red flame shot from the wings of the Frescos, stitching a path through the blue-green night.

"Going to ECM," Farnsworth responded as he started the electronic countermeasures to avoid the missiles.

It was then, as he started to hit the chaff/flare switch to spread a string of heat-emitting flares designed to draw the Frescos' missiles, that the worse of all possibilities rose like a bad dream.

A jolt shook the fighter.

An eerie, sickening silence enveloped the cockpit. Outside noise had fallen to a low, terrifying whisper.

Farnsworth felt his stomach tighten. "God in heaven," he mumbled to the back of Sacrette's helmet. "We've lost the starboard burner."

"Shut down the radar." Sacrette spoke quickly, reaching for the right side of the instrument panel. For the starboard engine extinguisher button.

A split second later the Hornet was totally without power.

In that same instant, five miles from their cockpit, two fireballs illuminated in their blue-green field of view. A bright orange flame licked at the sky as the Frescos disintegrated.

"Yeah!" Farnsworth shouted. "Anytime, baby! Anytime!"

For a moment both men forgot they were flying in a jetfighter that didn't have engine power.

Farnsworth saw the two missiles from the Fresco fly past harmlessly and only for that moment was he glad the engine heat source was cooling in the night air above the Cuban coast.

Then the reality set in.

"Damn, Thunderbolt," Farnsworth said softly. "We're . . ."

Before the CPO could finish his sentence, Sacrette finished it for him.

"Hang on to your ass, Chief. We're going down!"

2

WHILE MOST AIRCRAFT HAVE LONG-RANGE GLIDE CApability, a short-winged fighter with engine failure takes on the dimensions of a falling brick.

As the Hornet's airspeed indicator began bleeding off from the loss of power, Sacrette lowered the nose to gain airspeed, hoping to prevent stall departure.

Farnsworth tightened the chest strap on his torso harness connected to the SJU-5/A ejection seat. "Give the word when you're ready to eject, Thunderbolt. This bird's coming out of the sky like a stripped-assed ape!"

Shaking his head, Sacrette had already realized that the two men's fate was inextricably joined to that of the fighter. "No can do, Chief."

"What!" Farnsworth sounded like a man in pain.

"Look down there, Chief. That's Cuba. We can't eject. This aircraft is outfitted with classified night attack equipment. If the Cubes get their hands on the equipment, it'll be Moscow-bound by morning. We have to ride her in to the drink. We'll scuttle at sea. It's the only way."

"Are you crazy! You're going to make a no-engines landing at sea? In the dark?" Farnsworth was nearly standing in his seat.

Sacrette's voice grew firm. "That's my order, Chief Farnsworth. I'm the pilot. You're the passenger. I'm going to try for Gitmo. So sit your ass tight, and if you know any Top Twenty prayers, now is the perfect time to hear number one on the Hit Parade."

In the pit Farnsworth ripped off the night goggles; instantly his eyes were drowned in a sea of velvety pitch-blackness.

"God almighty. This is no way for a man to die!" he said, then quickly pulled the night goggles back over his eyes. Rivulets of sweat streaked from his shaved head, leaving a wet, filmy sheen that pooled into his thick mustache. His mouth tasted like copper, and although he was more scared than he could remember feeling, he suddenly began to grow calm.

A calm brought on by the blue-green figure flying the Hornet.

Holding the HOTAS, Sacrette calmly switched to a crypto frequency, then radioed the *Valiant*. "Home Plate, Wolf One turning to heading one-one-five. Both engines down. Making a run for Guantánamo. If we can't make Gitmo, will land in the sea."

"Roger, Wolf One." The voice of the young radio operator sounded as though it came from another dimension.

Glancing down, Sacrette watched the coast of Cuba off his left wing as he turned southeast, toward the American naval base at Guantánamo Bay.

"Get ready, Chief. We're going to get our feet wet," Sacrette ordered.

"Ready." It was all Farnsworth could think of to say.

Thinking about the aircraft, the classified night at-

tack equipment that might fall into Soviet hands, kept
Sacrette from thinking about death. His mind was turning with the speed of a locomotive, as he tried to figure
out what was the best plan. He could go in nose down,
destroying the Hornet on impact, but that wouldn't guar-
antee that the Cubans wouldn't find the wreckage. Or
that the cockpit wouldn't remain intact. He had seen
fighters crash before, and knew there was recoverable
wreckage.

He might reach Guantánamo, but noting his rate of
descent, and the horizon above him, the sea coming up
fast from below, he knew that reaching the naval base
was impossible.

Glancing out, he could see the water; and the Jardines de la Reina, a sprinkling of islands etching the
surface. Looking toward the coast, he saw a single outcropping, a finger of land jutting from the Communist
island.

"Christ!" he blurted. Switching on the FLIR, he
turned the nose toward the finger of land. Instantly the
FLIR was projecting a digital moving map on the right
digital display indicator. Fed by cathode ray tubes, the
DDI television screen gave a one-to-one ratio field of
view.

He reached instinctively and tapped the finger. He
remembered the name of that particular part of the island
known for its multicolored birds. "French Soldier's
Point!"

"What?" asked Farnsworth, who was quietly waiting
for his fate to be determined.

Sacrette knew why he remembered the Point.
Drawing a line from the Point toward the sea, he tapped
a spot that lay between the islands of Jardines de la Reina
and the coast of Cuba.

A round depression glowed prominently in the water. A depression made darker by its depth compared to that of the surrounding water.

"Perfect," he said aloud.

"What's perfect?" Farnsworth asked. "Ain't nothing perfect except a good-looking woman's ass . . . and if you see one of them I'd like a look. It might be the last good thing I'll ever see."

Sacrette shook his head. "Better than a good-looking woman's ass, Chief. A place to put this bird so nobody can find her. Except the people tracking us aboard the *Valiant*."

Farnsworth knew the ELT was transmitting their position in crypto; a signal that was being monitored by one of the surveillance satellites flying eighty miles above the Caribbean.

"What do you got in mind, Thunderman?"

Sacrette pointed to the depression as the Hornet passed over it. "Four miles from shore the shelf drops to several thousand feet. Between the shelf and the shore there's a spot where the water is deep enough to hide the Hornet from aerial observation. It's about a half mile wide. The storm will mask our landing. And I doubt any fishing boats are out on the water tonight. Including military craft. It's not much . . . but it's all we've got."

Sacrette's instincts took command. Instincts and leadership, coupled with responsibility for preventing a TOP SECRET aircraft from falling into the wrong hands.

"I'm going to fly toward the island, then swing back on a one-eighty. Cuban radar will think we've gone off the scope and boogied out of country above the water. When we hit, hold on tight. Don't do anything. Not a thing. No matter what you hear. Or what you see. Understand?"

Farnsworth didn't; but he didn't have any other choice except to place his trust in the CAG.

"It's your call, Commander Sacrette," Farnsworth replied solemnly.

Sacrette scanned the television screen where the cathode ray tubes fed a digital display of the depression. He memorized the display, then a flick of his finger shut down the emergency landing transmitter.

Sacrette pulled back on the HOTAS, whipping the low-flying Hornet into a 180-degree "bat-turn." The airspeed dropped to 150.

The Hornet was below Cuban radar, invisible to the satellite, and approaching the Gulf of Guacanayabo in a silence broken only by the steady whisper of the fighter dropping through the night.

Looking out the canopy, Sacrette saw the surface; whitecaps danced, ghostlike, through the blue-green field.

"Hang on, Chief!" Sacrette shouted. He went to full flaps, slowing the fighter as much as possible.

The Hornet touched the water at five miles above stall departure, then nosed forward, appearing to slide along the surface. Like a giant bird, the Hornet rose again into the air, hung there for a moment, then angled sharply toward the sea.

"The next one's for real," Sacrette called above the screeching noise of the metal finding resistance against the sea.

The second impact was worse than the initial contact. Impact that slammed both men into their seats, then jerked them forward; harness straps bit into their bodies, feet flew out, arms flailed, and breathing stopped completely.

Seconds later the aircraft settled, then began to drift down toward the dark reaches of the depression.

"Get the goggles off, Chief," Sacrette ordered.

Farnsworth felt the sickening descent of the Hornet begin. Through the canopy he could see the water closing around the Hornet.

"Sweet suffering Jesus," the CPO blurted. "When are we going to un-ass this bitch!"

Before he could get an answer, the Hornet was claimed by the sea. And the thick, interminable blackness of the abyss.

"Sit tight, Chief. You've got to hang in here with me. All the way. I know what I'm doing."

"I hope so. Christ. It's darker than a well digger's dick."

Through the darkness, Sacrette's voice calmly replied. "I'll take care of that."

Suddenly the cockpit glowed in dull orange as the magenta interior lights came on.

Sacrette's helmet was off. He unbuckled his harness, then turned to the black CPO.

Sacrette's bronze facial features framed two piercing blue eyes above a long, slender nose. Sweat dripped from his black hair. The rugged descendant of French-Canadian fur trappers radiated with intensity; yet there was a settling quality in his demeanor.

"What are we doing, Thunderman?"

"Finding out if we've got any juice." He reached to the instrument panel. A loud whirring was heard.

"You're lowering the landing gear?" Farnsworth said incredulously.

Without answering, Sacrette hit the external landing gear light as the gear locked into place.

"I don't believe my fucking eyes." As Farnsworth stared out of the cockpit, the world of inner space suddenly turned blue.

Taking the HOTAS, Sacrette talked fast. Like a man trying to explain something on the run.

"We're in a 'Blue Hole,' Chief. It's called the Blue Hole of Reina. Half mile wide. One hundred and fifty feet deep. I'm going to fly this baby onto the bottom. Then we'll get the hell out of here." He pointed to the coral wall outside the cockpit.

A myriad of colors splashed the coral wall constituting what was called a blue hole. A hole in otherwise shallow water, like a well sunk into a desert.

Orange Garibaldis swam in a large school, darting crazily as the jetfighter invader drifted downward. Marine life of every type could be seen inhabiting the wall.

Shaking his head, Farnsworth couldn't believe what was happening.

Sacrette worked the stick, using the aircraft's elevators the way an aquanaut would "fly" an undersea submersible.

"The same principles of flight apply to flying underwater," he told the Chief, who wasn't particularly interested.

Farnsworth was nearly beyond comprehending anything.

"What about air?" the chief snapped.

Sacrette leaned to the front of the cockpit while talking. "We're airtight. There's enough loose oxygen in here to keep us for at least ten minutes. Not to mention our oxygen masks. The aircraft is sealed in all vital compartments."

Slowly the Hornet drifted toward the bottom.

Working the controls with a fury Farnsworth had never seen in a man, Sacrette guided the fighter down, down, until he pointed at the bottom. "There!"

Looking out, Farnsworth saw the white sandy bottom of the blue hole.

Moments later the fighter touched bottom, bounced a few feet upward, then settled in the sand.

A veil of sand swirled around the cockpit, then settled, painting the wings white, as though the Hornet were sitting on a snowy airstrip.

A long silence followed. Neither man said a word. They stared at the abyss.

Finally, Farnsworth had to ask the obvious.

"How we going to get out? Call the auto club?"

Sacrette laughed. "I'm glad you've kept that crusty sense of humor. We'll blow the canopy and make a free ascent."

Farnsworth whistled. "I haven't made an ascent from one-fifty since I was in the SEALs."

Sacrette flashed a devilish grin. "I've never made an ascent from one-fifty."

Farnsworth knew it was time to add his expertise to the situation. Quickly he explained what Sacrette needed to know. "When we blow the canopy—if the charges work..."

"They'll work," Sacrette interrupted.

"... Take a deep breath, then start up. You have to maintain a constant stream of bubbles, otherwise the decreasing pressure will cause the compressed air in your lungs to overexpand. That'll pump air into your blood, and you'll be dead within minutes. Capice?"

Sacrette nodded. "Sure. Just like scuba diving."

"Right. Now... what the hell are we going to do

after we reach the surface. If we reach the surface . . ."

"We'll reach the surface. Alive," Sacrette interrupted again.

". . . then what? That ain't Panama City Beach out there. And the folks in these parts don't like tourists."

Again the Sacrette grin. "We'll cover that when we get there. Are you ready?"

Farnsworth turned his eyes up. "No. But what choice do I have? Unless I want to be found by archaeologists someday, sitting in this airplane that's been turned into a fishbowl."

"Let's get to it," Sacrette replied.

They began stripping off their gear. Boots. Flight suits. When down to their shorts, both men put their survival harnesses back on. They tied their boot laces together and hung them around their necks. Sacrette, who carried a Louisiana Lightning knife in a boot scabbard, tied the razor-sharp dagger to his laces. The flight suits were rolled into a ball, to be carried under an arm.

When ready, Sacrette pointed at the canopy jettison handle on the left side of the cockpit. "When I blow the canopy, all hell's going to break loose. Take a deep breath and head for the surface. Don't wait for me. I'll be up ahead."

"What about these?" Farnsworth held up the "Cat's Eye" goggles. "They could get blown out of the cockpit."

During the excitement Sacrette had completely forgotten the goggles.

He thought for a moment. "Put them on the helmet, and buckle the chin strap. We'll buckle the helmets to the ejection seats' lap belts."

Thirty seconds later they were both ready.

Gripping the canopy jettison handle, Sacrette glanced at Farnsworth, who simply nodded. With his free hand, he turned off the landing gear lights and the interior lights.

The blackness returned.

"Take a deep breath!" Sacrette shouted through the darkness.

Then . . .

Sacrette jerked back on the jettison handle!

3

A LOUD RUMBLE RIPPLED ALONG THE AIRTIGHT SEAL of the clamshell canopy.

As the canopy lifted off, the cockpit was swallowed by an explosion of rushing bubbles.

"Go . . . you bitch!" Farnsworth commanded the rising canopy as he disappeared in a sea of swirling, bone-chilling seawater.

Feeling as though he had been hit in the chest with a shovel, Sacrette took a deep breath as he disappeared.

Fighting the pain of the pressure that was nearly six times greater than on the surface—both men felt their eustachian tubes and sinus passages begin to collapse. Before their eardrums ruptured, they pinched off their noses and exhaled sharply, equalizing the pressure in their inner ears.

When the swirling bubbles settled, Sacrette flashed a "thumbs-up," then pushed off from the seat.

Farnsworth followed in his trail.

Upward they soared; their legs churned, driving them toward the surface they couldn't see.

But could feel, in its drawing, calling distance.

A thin trail of bubbles followed in their wake; bubbles slowly expelled from their lungs.

One hundred feet from the surface their legs began to ache. Gnawing, biting pain shot through their upper extremities.

Sacrette felt the water become warmer, though he didn't know his depth.

Thirty seconds into the ascent, Farnsworth's lungs began heaving as his blood pressure raced like a thoroughbred's fresh across the finish line.

Each man thrust an arm toward the surface—toward the sanctuary of the open sea.

The quiet was what Sacrette noticed above all. Except for the pounding of his heart. A pristine quiet that was both calming, and frightening.

At ten feet Sacrette thought he saw the moon. But there was no moon. The fury of Hugo had rid them of that beacon.

Their oxygen was running low, their bubbles exhausted. They felt the ache of wanting to breathe as the carbon dioxide build-up made their lungs convulse.

And then, when the end seemed so near, when it seemed there was nothing else to give, they exploded through the surface.

They said nothing. For several long minutes they gulped air into their lungs.

Fresh. Clean. Air.

Finally, with tired, agonizing arms, they inflated their survival vests.

Riding on a cushion of air, they floated on the surface.

In the distance, toward Cuba, the lights of a fishing village burned faintly.

Farnsworth looked out to sea. Then toward Cuba. Though he was certain he knew the answer, he whispered to Sacrette. "Which way, Thunderbolt?"

Sacrette's arm came out of the water. A wet finger pointed toward another finger.

A finger of land jutting from the rocky coast.

"There. French Soldier's Point."

4

2200.

Joaquin Zarante sat in the passenger compartment of an eight-seat seaplane, his honey-brown features glowing momentarily in the silver-gold wash of a lightning flash. His was the classic face of the Huallagian Indian: long nose, thick lips, high eyebrows, and narrow cheekbones framed around black, oval eyes.

Expensive clothes offset the cruelty of his face. His long, black hair, bound in a tight ponytail by a solid gold clasp bearing two crossed machettes, hung well beyond the collar of his Thierry Mugler double-breasted wool-crepe sport coat. His shoes were from Lorenzo Banfi; silk shirt from L'Zinger.

The shoulder holster beneath his coat was Bianchi; the 9mm automatic pistol resting in the holster was by Beretta.

Sipping cognac, he paused as he heard the engines throttle back; then came the whirr of the electric flaps rolling beneath the wing outside the window.

Checking his watch, he was pleased. The schedule was being kept.

Below, the choppy water of the Gulf of Guacanayabo rose and fell beneath the throes of the hurricane, but

Zarante didn't seem to mind.

Feeling the sensation of banking as the airplane turned onto its upwing approach to landing, he reached between his feet and hoisted a briefcase onto his lap.

Opening the case, he smiled. He always smiled when reminded of the power he now so easily wielded.

Inside the briefcase two million dollars lay beneath a small bottle.

Removing the bottle, he loosened the cap, then poured a tiny sprinkling of white powder onto one of the stacks of bills lying in the briefcase. A quick snort, then the warm, glowing rush of the cocaine flooded his senses.

He laughed.

He was ready to conduct his business.

5

2230.

CUCHO CLEMENTE SLID QUIETLY INTO THE SURGING tide of the cove. Wearing nothing but shorts, he swam toward the open sea. In a matter of seconds he was beyond the view of the Diaz brothers, who stood on the beach.

He paused thirty yards from shore. Looking up, he could see the thin outline of the rocky outcropping where the blond man had stood. Slowly he allowed his eyes to follow the imaginary path of the globe's arc toward the water.

Swimming to the point where he believed the globe had disappeared, he threw his legs back, bent at the waist, and disappeared.

A silty, drifting cloud of sand greeted him, stinging his eyes, filling his pockets, stripping him of all sense of direction. But he knew the bottom was there. Somewhere. The problem would be searching the bottom with such poor visibility.

Groping like a blind man, he felt along the sandy bottom.

Nothing.

Time and again he repeated the dive, each time

coming up with nothing, except a growing fatigue. In-
termittently he would try to rest on the surface, but
against the pulling surge, the pauses only made him more
tired.

Again he re-created the last moments of the dead
man's life.

He saw the globe. The arc. The splash.

Each time the ball-like . . .

Ball!

His mind shouted.

"Stupido," his whispered to himself. "It was shaped
like a ball. A ball will roll."

He thought for a moment. Three days had passed
since the incident with the blond man and the soldiers.

He saw the motioning arm of the blond man that
came nightly to his bed. He heard the roar of the helicopters. The thunder of the exploding grenade.

His sleep had been filled with the memory.

During the day he and the Diaz brothers had
watched from the trees while soldiers combed every inch
of the beach. For what he wasn't certain. He suspected
they wanted the ball thrown by the blond man.

As did Cucho. It had become a game between play-
ers.

Who would catch the ball?

He became motionless. The surge of the incoming
tide pushed him toward shore. His mind began to drift,
the best way he knew to fight pain. Fatigue.

He began to reconstruct that day. The brothers were
in the shoreline. The tide was out.

His brain began calculating from a formula learned
in childhood by all of the children raised on the sea.

Every six hours the tide changes. Three hours of

tide rolling out to sea. Three hours of tide rolling toward shore. And the hurricane.

Shore!

The roll against the inclining beach would meet greater resistance. The least resistance would be toward the sea.

The ball would roll toward the sea!

He looked toward the sea.

Playing a hunch, he swam away from the shore.

The tide towed him away from the beach, allowing him to rest while he tried to think of the best place to search. He wasn't concerned about returning to the beach, or whether the ball would be too heavy. His thoughts were only on the ball.

And its possession.

He dove again. Groping in the sand, he surfaced with nothing but seeping granules.

Again he dove. Then again. Each time he surfaced with nothing.

Finally, feeling the biting agony of defeat, he wanted to quit.

"No," he shouted. "I must not quit."

He dove again. His lungs ached. His eyes burned from the salty water. But suddenly, without thinking, he found the strength for another dive, and disappeared from the surface.

On the bottom Cucho kicked and stroked against the outgoing bottom surge until he felt the energy pass. Then he relaxed, floating along inches off the bottom of an incoming surge.

As his lungs ached, and he started to surface, he felt something touch his fingers.

Digging his fingers into the sand, he clawed savagely, and then felt the object again.

He thought his lungs would burst as his fingers felt something round, then pulled the object to where it touched his nose.

It was too dark to see, yet somehow he knew he had found what the blond man had died to keep from the soldiers.

"The ball!" he shouted, spilling precious air from his lungs. "The ball."

Moments later he recovered his composure. The globe was smooth, heavier than he imagined. Slowly he pulled himself toward the surface.

Swimming toward the Diaz brothers, he carried the shiny globe like some great trophy.

"You found it," Alessandro Diaz whispered excitedly.

"Yes," said Juan. "But what did you find?" He reached and touched the sphere. "I have never seen a baseball made of steel."

"Come," said Cucho. A chill raced along his spine. He looked around. "We must go. The soldiers might return."

They slipped quietly from the beach, moving like young jungle cats along a trail that led toward their village.

6

2330.

JOAQUIN ZARANTE FOLLOWED A CUBAN SOLDIER through a ribbon wire-topped fence; beyond the fence, two soldiers patrolled along the side of a long, rectangular-shaped concrete building set deep into the jungle floor.

Glancing up, Zarante saw the building was protected by a canopy of overhanging trees. Beyond the building, a military complex sat equally hidden, lit only by the glow of a few soft blue lights.

Entering the building, a thick smell struck his nostrils: pungent, bitter, but, he thought to himself, a rewarding smell. A saving smell.

He was shown to a room where he sat on a wooden chair; the furnishings were Spartan, unlike the lavish surroundings of his villa in the jungle near Tingo Maria.

He turned as a heavy door opened. Two men entered. Both were smiling.

Colonel Raol Escobar, a short, thin soldier, nodded politely, then extended his hand. He wore fatigues, his ferret face nearly lost within a carpet of curly, twisting facial hair.

Zarante almost laughed, as he nearly did the first

time they met. The man looked like a shortened, malnutritioned version of Fidel Castro. "Senor Zarante. Welcome back to Campo Viramo." Escobar offered a bony hand that was lost in Zarante's massive grip.

The second man was taller. Heavyset. A European. His thick, pudgy fingers were constantly moving.

Zarante bowed politely, then shook hands with Dorffman.

Seating himself, he looked at Dorffman. "You seem nervous, Herr Doctor. Is everything going as planned?"

Dorffman wiped at the sweat on his forehead with the cuff of the white smock he wore. "Of course. The project is nearing completion."

Zarante looked at Escobar. The colonel nodded. "Then you have prepared a demonstration?"

Escobar glanced at the briefcase. "You have brought the second installment?"

Zarante took the briefcase and handed it to Escobar.

As Escobar started to open the valise, he saw Zarante's right eyebrow arch slowly.

"I am sure you have provided the correct amount." Escobar smiled thinly, then placed the briefcase on a table in the corner.

"The demonstration?" Zarante asked flatly.

Rising, Escobar motioned to the heavy door. "This way, Senor Zarante."

Following the two men, Zarante was led into a small room where he was immediately met by the shrieks and screams of dozens of rhesus monkeys held in metal cages anchored to long tables.

Walking to the rear of the room, Dorffman opened the thick door of a glass-enclosed cage.

"Would you care to select the specimen?" Escobar

asked Zarante while nodding at the cages.

Zarante said nothing; going to the cages, he carefully scanned the howling monkeys.

"How are you, my pretty," Zarante whispered to a monkey. The monkey was the only one not howling; instead, the creature bared his fangs defiantly.

"You should use this glove, Senor Zarante," suggested Escobar, whose extended hand clutched a heavy leather glove.

Zarante chuckled. He opened the cage, held his left hand to the monkey. As the monkey charged his left hand, Zarante's right hand flashed at the monkey's throat.

Zarante pulled the monkey from the cage and walked to the glass enclosure. As Dorffman stepped out of the way of the kicking, flailing rhesus, Zarante shoved the animal through the door.

Sealing the door closed, Dorffman went to a safe built into the concrete wall. He removed a metallic box. Carefully he raised the lid of the box. Six holes were machined into the box; four holes were occupied by tiny vials.

Zarante noticed the two empty holes. "Where are the other two vials?"

Dorffman shrugged. "We conducted a further experiment yesterday. To make certain of the dosage. We wanted the demonstration to be perfect."

Zarante's eyelids tightened at the corners. A long, uneasy pause followed. Finally, Zarante smiled lightly. But his eyes remained tight with suspicion.

Motioning to the glass box, Zarante told Dorffman, "You may now demonstrate what my ten-million-dollar investment has produced."

7

2345.

REACHING THE SMALL CABANA WHERE CUCHO LIVED with the Diaz family, the boys slipped through the window into the room they shared.

They sat on the dirt floor in a circle. Cucho set the ball in the center. Holding a single candle for light, Alessandro looked disappointed at the globe. "It is too heavy. We cannot use the ball to play baseball. We will have to use coconuts."

Juan picked up the ball. His fingers felt a thin seam in the sphere's circumference. "It is cracked," he said disappointedly. "One hit with the bat and it would break apart."

Dropping the sphere on the floor, the boys looked heartbroken.

Several moments passed. Finally, Cucho took the sphere. Holding the globe to the candlelight, he examined the crack.

A perfect line was etched around the center of the globe. An idea materialized.

Carefully he twisted the top half clockwise, while twisting the lower half counterclockwise. He felt the two hemispheres move.

He repeated the motion, and the sphere separated into two halves.

Juan gasped. "What is it, Cucho?"

Cucho shook his head. "I don't know."

Centered in each hemisphere was a countersunk nut; a thin screwdriver groove was machined into each nut.

"Give me your knife," Cucho said to Alessandro.

Opening the knife, he turned the screw until it began threading out of the hemisphere. Once out, they saw a cylindrical hole had been machined into the hemisphere.

Inside the cylindrical hole rested what none could recognize.

"What is it?" Alessandro asked excitedly.

Cucho dumped the hemisphere into the palm of his hand. A tiny glass vial fell onto his palm.

"What is it?" Alessandro asked again.

Cucho shrugged. "Some kind of bottle."

"There must be another in the other half," Alessandro surmised.

Alessandro took the vial and held it to the candlelight. "There is something inside the bottle."

The vial contained a colorless liquid.

"It looks like water," Alessandro said.

Cucho shook his head. "Why would the blond man put water in the glass?"

Juan snatched the vial from Alessandro, and in doing so squeezed too hard.

The sound of breaking glass echoed from his hand.

Juan sat forward, holding his hand to the light. Blood began to flow in the web between his thumb and index finger.

Alessandro's hand shot out to his bleeding brother. The wet liquid, mixed with his brother's blood, dripped onto Alessandro's skin.

Suddenly Juan bolted upright, nearly snapping his spine.

A loud ringing burst in his head. His eyes bulged; his lips twisted his mouth grotesquely. He tried to scream, but the muscles of his face were frozen.

"Juan!" Alessandro shouted over the buzz saw ringing that was now mounting in his skull. He jerked spastically onto his belly; twisting, rolling, his feet thrashing uncontrollably.

Cucho jumped to his feet. The brothers were flopping about like fish dumped to the floor of their boat.

A white, milky spittle drooled from Juan's mouth. Then from Alessandro's.

In what Cucho could only describe as something from the devil, the two boys' faces suddenly swelled like giant watermelons.

Their eyes disappeared beneath swollen lids; their mouths became nothing more than slits.

High-pitched screams gurgled from their throats. Thrashing. Flopping. Grunting. The spittle turned to blood, and then they both grabbed at their throats.

Horrified, Cucho stepped back, not certain what to do. "They are choking," he said aloud.

A clammy hand suddenly reached toward Cucho. Looking down, he saw the purpling face of Alessandro staring up at him. He looked like a newborn pup, close-eyed, searching for his mother's teat.

Remembering what had happened to Alessandro after he touched his brother, Cucho jumped away from the reaching boyhood friend.

Both boys issued a guttural noise. Deep. Chilling. As though from hell.

Suddenly Juan jerked, then lay motionless.

Alessandro pitched forward onto his face. A sudden release of air followed as he expelled a long, sickening gasp.

Frightened beyond belief, Cucho ran to the window.

"Run! Run!" his mind commanded.

He hit the ground in a full sprint, not wanting to look back. The shame of leaving his friends burned him with every step. The images of their twisted faces danced before his eyes, spurring his escape from that place of what he could only think of as . . . evil!

In a flash he disappeared into the heavy foliage of the black jungle.

In his hands, gripped by muscles taut with panic, he clutched the two halves of the sphere.

One half empty.

The other half still holding whatever demon had been created at La Casa del Diablo.

8

0045.

"I DIDN'T THINK THOSE DAMN KIDS WOULD EVER leave," Farnsworth grumped. He was sitting in the deep, lush foliage of the jungle. Fifty meters away, the wind from the approaching hurricane was turning the cove into a choppy tempest.

Sacrette untied the laces of his flight boots. "They must have been nuts. Swimming at night in storm surge. Did you see that one kid? He kept diving for something."

Farnsworth remembered watching the boy, afraid he might discover the aviators floating toward shore. "That was close, Thunder. Damn close."

Diamonds rubbed his face. Prickly stings of pain raced from his ears to his throat. His face was swollen; ears and sinuses ached.

As did Sacrette's.

Dressed in their flight suits, they pulled their boots on slowly. Checking his watch, Sacrette realized he had been awake for nearly twenty-four hours. Fatigue was setting in.

"What's our next move, Thunderbolt?" Farnsworth asked.

Sacrette thought for a moment. A mental display of

---

the island projected in his brain. Carefully he studied the mental hologram.

"We've got two choices." Pointing southeast, he laid out the situation. "We're approximately fifty miles from Gitmo . . . by land. Twenty-five by sea. Straight across the gulf."

Farnsworth shook his head. "That's a long swim. And traveling fifty miles through enemy terrain isn't much better."

"It's all we have, Chief," Sacrette said flatly. "We dropped two Cuban airplanes tonight, Diamonds. I wouldn't expect leniency if we turn ourselves in to the local authorities."

"Yeah," Diamonds responded thoughtfully. "We'll get a reception of blowtorches and pliers. The notion of my chestnuts roasting on an open fire—while being skinned alive—isn't my idea of dying peacefully."

"I say we take the sea route."

Diamonds whistled softly. "Man. Have you forgotten there's a hurricane rolling in this direction?"

"No. I haven't. We can use the storm for cover. The hurricane won't be here for two days. By then, we'll be tucked in safe and sound at the BOQ."

Farnsworth wasn't convinced. "What about a boat?"

Sacrette threw his head toward the west. "There's a fishing village a few miles from here. We'll lay low during the day, then slip in later tonight. A boat won't be missed. Not during a storm. Between here and Guantánamo is the Golfo de Guacanayabo. The Gulf of Guacanayabo. We'll head straight across the gulf."

Farnsworth could see there wasn't much choice. "We'd better get some shut-eye. I have a feeling we're looking at a long day. And night."

Sacrette agreed. "You get some sleep. I'll take the first watch."

Taking several heavy palm fronds torn from trees, the two sailors covered their bodies, where they lay hidden in silence.

Farnsworth fell fast asleep. Fighting the need to close his eyes, Sacrette began playing a mental game he had learned in survival training.

He began at his toes, working each joint, each muscle, from his feet to his head. Reaching his neck, which ached from the impact of landing, he started back down to his toes.

As he began repeating the game, which kept him concentrating on a specific physical act, while keeping his mind occupied, he felt the hair stand on the nape of his neck.

Turning, he thought he sensed movement.

He saw nothing. Returning to the game, he repeated the process, not noticing the slight, almost imperceptible movement from the branches twenty feet above.

Looking down from his swaying perch, Cucho Clemente stared in total fascination at the two Americanos.

In his hands he was still clutching the sphere that had killed his two friends.

9

"YOUR DEMONSTRATION WAS SUPERB, DR. DORFF-man. As anticipated." Looking first at the dead monkey in the glass box, then at Dorffman, Joaquin Zarante was smiling in the same demented way the European had seen tortured political prisoners smile in Soviet "psychiatric" hospitals.

The smile of a raving lunatic.

Only in this case, a smart lunatic. And very dangerous. With the power and money to reach beyond government boundaries, including Cuba. And East Germany.

"Thank you, Senor Zarante." Dorffman was growing more frightened by the moment. The man's eyes seemed to see through his fear. Seemed to know that they had violated the security of the facility by losing two of the vials to that goddamned traitor!

Checking his solid gold Gucci watch, Zarante started for the door. "I must return to Montego Bay. I have business to conduct there in the morning. Banking business."

Escobar grinned. "Excellent. I shall tell the generalissimo that you are satisfied with your investment."

"Yes." Zarante looked very pleased. "You have used my money well. We will be able to rid ourselves of many problems." He laughed wickedly. "Perhaps buy ourselves a new country."

The ringing of a telephone on the wall caught their attention. Escobar answered, listened carefully, then hung up without speaking.

"Problems?" Zarante asked, noticing the pale look on Escobar's face.

"No problem, Senor Zarante. One of my men molested a young woman in the village tonight. I shall have to deal with him."

Zarante laughed. "We are all accountable, Colonel Escobar. I, too, must discipline my people. I, too, am accountable to the people in my organization. You and I, we are in a business that allows no mistakes. No mercy."

"This is true." Escobar was looking coldly at Dorffman.

Zarante clapped his hands loudly. "It is time to leave. I understand you will have a sufficient quantity prepared within forty-eight hours. Is that correct?" He was looking at Dorffman.

Dorffman nodded. "The process time is about two liters per day. I can have four liters prepared for you within forty-eight hours."

Zarante looked pleased. "Four liters. That will be enough. Enough for what I plan to do with your first delivery."

"May I ask what you intend to do?" Escobar asked.

Zarante grumped slightly. "No. But I can tell you this . . . everything is in place for the first 'message' to be delivered the day after I pick up the chemicals. A great deal of planning and preparation has gone into the first message." He looked sternly at the men. "You must not fail. It is very important you have the four liters when I return in two nights."

"We will have your first batch, Senor Zarante," said Escobar.

They shook hands, then Zarante left for the jeep that would drive him to the waiting seaplane.

When Zarante had left Camp Viramo, Escobar turned to Dorffman. His eyes blazed as he said, "I have located the vials stolen by the KGB agent."

10

Battle Group Zulu Station, South of Jamaica. 0115.

"TEN-HUT!"

The sharp bark of a young officer echoed through the ready room of the USS *Valiant*, snapping the sleepy-eyed squadron commanders of the carrier's air wing to their feet in the front two rows.

Seven squadron commanders where there would normally be eight; the only squadron commander missing was Commander Boulton Sacrette, who not only served as the CAG, but as squadron commander of the Strike/Fighter squadron.

In the rear several pilots from VFA-101, the air wing's F/A-18 a*V*iation *F*ighter *A*ttack squadron, were the first to see the battle group commander enter.

From where he sat in the front row, Lt. Commander Anthony "Domino" Dominolli, the VFA-101 squadron exec. noticed that Captain Elrod Lord's shoulders, which he generally carried like square-rigged sails, seemed to sag beneath a heavy burden.

It was no secret. They had known since four hours earlier, when the word had spread through the carrier like wildfire:

The Thunderbolt was down!

"Gentlemen. Here's an update on Commander Sacrette and CPO Farnsworth. Search and rescue operations were planned for this morning, based on meteorology predictions that hurricane Hugo would change to a northwesterly course after passing through Puerto Rico. Hugo has changed course."

Lord took a deep breath. The pilots could see Hugo's course wasn't all that had changed. Then Lord kicked them in the gut.

"The Pentagon has suspended all search and rescue operations for Commander Sacrette."

A low growl rumbled through the ready room.

"That's bullshit! Sir!" jumping to his feet, Lt. Darrel "Blade" Blaisedale shouted disrespectfully to the captain. His normally soft, polite Texas drawl rang like hardened steel.

Lord's laser-green eyes locked onto Lt. Blaisedale. As though joined by a beam, Lord's stare guided the young pilot back into his seat.

"I agree," Lord said dejectedly.

"What's the skinny, Captain?" Domino asked.

Lord took a deep breath. "Commander Sacrette's aircraft was outfitted with the night attack equipment. Surveillance satellite tracking and communication monitoring, as well as reports from operatives inside Cuba, indicate the Cubans are unaware that Commander Sacrette has gone down inside Cuban territory."

"In other words," Blade blurted sarcastically, "if we mount a search, the Cubes will get suspicious. They might find *Double Nuts*."

Blade was referring to the name given the CAG's aircraft, whose aircraft number always ended in a double zero.

"That's correct," Lord replied. "Commander Sacrette engaged two aircraft with hostile intent. Granted, it was over Cuban airspace. However, due to the circumstances, and the sensitive nature of Sacrette's aircraft, the Joint Chiefs feel Commander Sacrette made the proper move. It's up to the State Department and government to iron out the political ramifications."

"In the meanwhile, what do we do, sir? Sit on our lard?" Lt. Commander Hunter Frost spoke up. Tall, blond, a younger-looking version of Paul Newman, he had just arrived aboard the *Valiant* from China Lake.

Frost was the newly assigned commander of the SH-60B Seahawk antisubmarine warfare (ASW) helicopter squadron. He and Sacrette had served and worked together during Operation Urgent Fury when the US invaded Grenada.

"We'll maintain one Alert Five force, buckled in and ready to launch. The rest of the wing will conduct standard ops, which, I remind you, is to assist the Coast Guard and DEA in drug interdiction."

A rumble of discontent shook the ready room.

Captain Lord nodded at Domino. "Lt. Commander Dominolli, you'll assume the responsibilities of the VFA-101 squadron commander. I'll assume responsibilities of the CAG."

Saying nothing else, Lord walked from the podium, leaving the pilots to vent their anger and frustration without his presence.

An anger and frustration he felt himself, but, due to command, could not vent openly.

Reaching his sea cabin, the captain's private quarters near the bridge, Lord slumped into the chair at his desk. Glancing around the walls, he saw several photographs of airplanes he had flown since Korea.

One particular photograph caught his eye.

A young flight officer was sitting in the cockpit of a F-4 Phantom on the carrier USS *Nimitz*, the main attack platform of the Yankee Station battle group off the coast of Viet Nam.

He suddenly let out a laugh as he stared at Lt. j.g. Boulton Sacrette. Not at Sacrette himself, but at what was sitting on his shoulder.

A chimpanzee. Whom Sacrette affectionately labeled with the "running name" of Martini. Sacrette had landed aboard the *Nimitz* with a monkey, then had proceeded to become a legend with VF-84 in the skies over North and South Viet Nam.

That was the day Lord, who had been the VF-84 "Jolly Rogers" squadron commander and *Nimitz*'s CAG, discovered his first gray hair.

11

0215.

THE ROAR OF JEEPS PIERCED THE NIGHT, RIPPING from a deep sleep the villagers of Santa Rosa. Flashing lights danced off the adobe walls, casting long, eerie red and blue shadows against the glass windows, where many villagers watched wide-eyed as trucks filled with soldiers ground through the muddy streets.

Thoughts of many villagers snapped back through the decades, to another night such as this, causing them to wonder if another invasion was unfolding, like the day at Bahía de Cochinos—the Bay of Pigs.

Colonel Raol Escobar dismounted from the lead jeep, his black eyes slowly examining the village, a shithole reminiscent of his childhood in a similar village on the north coast.

Before Castro. And the Revolución. Where he found his destiny in the rugged mountains as a runner for Che Guevara.

Now, at forty-five, he was district commissioner of the Directorio de Gobierno Información. The Directory of Government Information. Known by the initials DGI.

To others, especially its tortured victims, it was simply called the "Directory."

Cuban Intelligence.

As the local *el jara* approached, Escobar studied the frightened willow of a man walking at the policeman's side.

Antonio Diaz wore the look, and walked, like a man who had seen the devil. Whimpering, head down, he was half dragged by the policeman, who appeared as confused as the fisherman.

"Colonel Escobar. This is the father." The policeman pulled Diaz around to face Escobar.

"Where are the bodies?" Escobar asked in a voice void of pity, or compassion.

Whimpering, Diaz turned and walked toward his cabana. At that moment Dorffman stepped from the jeep and followed Escobar.

Dorffman walked like a man about to face the firing squad.

As they stepped through the doorway, Escobar and Dorffman recognized the veil of miasma that stung their nostrils. It was a smell that permeated the testing laboratories at Campo Viramo, the secret facility known by the villagers as La Casa del Diablo.

Escobar covered his nose with a handkerchief. Slowly he went to the bodies lying on the floor. They no longer looked human. Their faces were gone, obscured by swelling; their hands and feet were swollen clumps, like sides of smoked ham.

After a quick examination of the bodies, Dorffman nodded to Escobar. "Your suspicions were correct, Colonel Escobar."

"Are you certain, Dr. Dorffman?" Escobar snapped.

Dorffman shrugged. "I will need my laboratory to make a conclusive examination. However, there is one way we can be reasonably certain."

Removing a scalpel from his coat, Dorffman cut along the wrist of Alessandro Diaz; a deep, circular cut that nearly severed the hand from the arm.

"Satisfied?" Dorffman asked, pointing at the severed wrist.

Glancing at the wrist, Escobar saw what was missing. "There is no blood."

Dorffman nodded. "Total coagulation. Their blood is like gelatin. I have no doubt they were infected with the Y-Karolin virus."

Escobar slowly turned, examining the room. Nodding, he reaffirmed what Dorffman suspected. "The boys found the sample stolen by your assistant, Hans Wagner. The KGB informant."

"Obviously," Dorffman replied.

Slowly Escobar's diamond black eyes began roaming the room. Momentarily, they paused on something that was sprinkled beneath Juan Diaz's body.

Using the toe of his boot, Escobar pushed the boy over, as though he were carrion.

Bits of broken glass glittered in the pale light.

Kneeling, Dorffman carefully examined the glass without touching the body.

"One of the vials," he said flatly.

"I only see one of the containers. There were two vials," Escobar said, looking at Antonio Diaz.

The man's eyes rose in ignorance. "I know nothing. Perhaps you should ask Cucho."

"Who is Cucho?" the DGI colonel snapped.

"Cucho Clemente. An orphan boy who lived with us since the death of his family. They were like brothers."

"Where is Cucho Clemente?" Escobar demanded in a voice like the wind howling from the approaching hurricane.

Diaz shook his head. He said nothing.

Escobar's hand flashed from his side. His powerful, bony fingers gripped Diaz by the wrist. A vicious twist followed, turning Diaz's hand toward his elbow, trapping the medial nerve between the bones of the wrist. On the back of Diaz's hand, Escobar's thumb dug into the radial nerve between the index and middle finger.

Dropping to his knees, Diaz screamed, a long, howling, undulating scream as Escobar worked the nerve with his thumb.

"Where is the boy!" Escobar shouted.

Diaz shook his head. "He is gone."

"Where!" Escobar brought his arm up, still gripping the wrist, then drove the fisherman's elbow against his rising knee.

A sharp *crack* sounded over the man's screams.

Diaz's other arm was pointing toward the window. "The jungle. They play in the jungle. Near the cove." Spittle ran from his mouth; his eyes were open, two throbbing orbs reflecting a painful truthfulness.

Wheeling, Escobar left the room, marching toward his jeep. In his trail, the sergeant and Dorffman tried to keep pace.

At the jeep he took a microphone from a radio mounted on the dash. He spoke quickly, then dropped the mike in the seat. Motioning for Dorffman, the European stepped forward.

They said nothing with words; only with their eyes. Turning to the sergeant, Escobar gave his order.

"Burn the village. Everything. Especially the Diaz

house. You have fifteen minutes. Load the villagers into the trucks. Transport them to Campo Viramo."

"What about the father? He knows about the chemical? And the *constabularia*? The Peruvian insisted on absolute secrecy," Dorffman reminded Escobar.

The DGI colonel turned to the sergeant. "Kill the father, and the *constabularia*."

As he started to get into the jeep, Escobar paused. He looked at the village. The face of Joaquin Zarante flashed in his mind.

Escobar looked at the sergeant. "Kill them all. Including the villagers!"

12

0515.

CAPTAIN LORD LAY IN HIS BUNK, STARING AT THE GRAY walls of his sea cabin. He was still dressed in his uniform, his tired eyes reflecting the despair flooding the souls of the more than sixty-five hundred men aboard the USS *Valiant*.

Sitting up, he reached for his pipe, then froze as a metallic voice blared, interrupting the stillness over the 1-MC intercom. The carrier's intercom system.

"Captain Lord. Report to the CIC. Urgent."

The combat information center, the nerve center of the *Valiant* during a combat situation, was behind the bridge. Passing a marine guard as he entered the bridge, Lord saluted, then strode into the CIC, where he was swamped by the glow of red lights illuminating the CIC.

Lt. Milt Floren, the carrier's chief intelligence cartography analyst, was a balding, stout descendant of southern slaves. A former PAC-10 running back at Washington State, he was sitting at a computer console. Above the console, a television screen projected a color digital display of the Caribbean.

As Floren looked up, a smile filled his black face. "I think I've got something, Captain."

Lord nodded.

Darker objects appeared as the screen seemed to move backward, revealing what Lord recognized as a chain of islands.

"That's the island group Jardines de la Reina. Off the southern coast of Cuba," Lord said flatly.

Floren nodded at the screen. "I've been here all night, Captain. Me and *LaCrosse* have eyeballed every inch of Cuba, and the Caribbean water surrounding the island. Nothing. Which made me suspicious. The satellite *LaCrosse* could find a tick on Castro's beard, if there was one."

"Go ahead," Lord said cautiously.

"That made me think. If there's no Cuban search vessels on the surface, and Commander Sacrette's last heading was toward Cuba, he must have gone down over land. If that's the case, why haven't we found signs of wreckage? At least a heat source from impact. Since he was flying a highly classified aircraft . . . we were tracking him by satellite the minute he left CONUS for the *Valiant*."

Pointing at the screen, he put his finger on the east island of the Reinas. "Commander Sacrette went off the scope here . . . inbound to Cuba. Which didn't make sense."

Lord agreed. "He would have known the best means of preventing the aircraft from falling into Cuban hands was to go into the drink."

"Exactly." Floren was nodding while looking at the screen. "Yet there's no search craft on the surface."

Lord shrugged. "They don't know he went down."

"Correct. Now . . . look at this. When Commander Sacrette went inbound to Cuba, he was at approximately five hundred feet, that's when he went off the screen. When he passed into the coast region of Cuba. At that altitude, he was obscured by ground clutter. Tracking downrange, figuring his rate of descent, flaps full, and so forth, he should have impacted two to three miles inside Cuban territory."

"You said you scanned every inch of that terrain."

Floren nodded. "For eight eyeball-burning hours. After which, I concluded he didn't go down over land."

Lord nodded methodically. He reached to the screen. "He flew low to throw Cuban radar off, then hooked a one-eighty back to sea."

"Precisely. But where is the aircraft? Plotting airspeed and altitude, he should have landed in the more shallow areas here." Floren drew a finger along a line extending from French Soldier's Point to the deeper water off the southern coast.

"Which you scanned. And found nothing."

A grin cut across Floren's face. "Almost."

"Explain," Lord ordered.

"I couldn't find anything in the shallow water. A bust. Then I noticed this depression, the Blue Hole of Reina."

Saying nothing more, Floren focused the cloud-penetrating laser eye of *LaCrosse* from eighty miles up to the Blue Hole of Reina.

Lord saw the hole turn darker blue against the surrounding water.

Moving closer, Lord's eyes narrowed on a darker object inside the outline of the hole. A single, fuzzy, almost imperceptible outline sitting on what Lord figured was the bottom of the Blue Hole of Reina.

"Good God!" Lord breathed heavily. "It's Sacrette's aircraft."

Floren slapped the top of the screen. "Yes, sir. He put her in the hole. But first, he shut down the emergency landing transmitter."

Lord shook his head. "He was thinking about security all the way to the end. He turned off the ELT so the Cubes couldn't pick up the signal."

Floren's voice suddenly sounded with gloom. "Nor could we, sir."

Lord's face turned to a mask of pain, although his eyes burned with an intense pride.

Tapping the screen softly, Lord was deep in thought. Finally, he spoke, saying what neither man had dared suggest.

"The aircraft is obviously intact, Lieutenant."

"Yes, sir. And the ELT's been turned off." Floren's voice was no more than a whisper.

"Which means they might have gotten out."

"Yes, sir. Damn good chance. It's a long way to the surface. But..." His voice faded into silence.

Drawing a finger across the Gulf of Guacanayabo, Lord stopped abruptly on the naval base at Guantánamo.

"If they made it to shore . . . they'll make for Guantánamo."

"My thoughts exactly."

Lord thought for a moment. A plan was developing. One that could end in disaster, but if successful, could make Commander Sacrette's decision to land in the hole that much more logical.

Turning to the red telephone hanging from the satellite communications scrambler, he ordered, "Get me the Pentagon."

The red telephone would take his message, encode the words in crypto, transmit them to a receiver via satellite to the Pentagon, and would then decode the message to the waiting operator.

Within seconds Lord was talking to the Joint Chiefs in the Pentagon.

"We've found Commander Sacrette's aircraft."

There was a response, then Captain Lord took a deep breath and said solemnly, "I believe the aircraft is recoverable."

13

1100.

SACRETTE HEARD THE RUMBLING OF TRUCKS, FOL-
lowed by shouts. The rattle of weaponry punctured the
stillness of the jungle, wrenching him from a restless
sleep.

His head ached; his eyes throbbed from the damage
caused by the tremendous squeeze during their escape
from the hole.

Jerking upright, he turned to Farnsworth. The vision made his skin crawl. Mucus was caked on his eyelids, yet he could see the CPO through the crusty haze.

"Diamonds," Sacrette whispered.

Farnsworth sat against a tree. He was facing Sacrette.

"Christ," Sacrette breathed heavily while crawling
to the black man.

"I can't see, Thunderman." His fingers touched at
his eyes. The lids were clamped shut by swelling. "I'm
blind, man." His ears turned to the voices shouting in
the distance.

"Get out of here, Thunder. Save yourself. I'll tell
them I survived. That you went down with the bird."

Sacrette's voice went cold. "Get up off your black

ass, sailor. We both go. Or we both stay."

Farnsworth shook his head. Sacrette grabbed the CPO by the collar of his flight suit, jerking him to his feet.

"We both go," he hissed in a whispering voice.

"Shit, man. You got to be in pain yourself. It's the blind leading the blind. We can't make it," Farnsworth's voice implored.

Taking Farnsworth by the arm, Sacrette began pulling the blinded chief.

Following a narrow trail leading away from the voices, Sacrette used the instincts honed during his youth while trapping in the Rockies of Montana; instincts handed down from generations of hearty mountain trappers who eluded Indians, rampaging grizzly bears, and thieving bandits.

The ground was sandy, wet from the rain, which he noticed had stopped. The sky was clear, suggesting that the hurricane might have changed course.

A thought he found unsettling. He had planned to use the hurricane as cover to make their way to Guantánamo.

Now, they would have to make the journey the old-fashioned way: through stealth, cunning, and the greatest of all motivators—the will to survive.

Fading slightly, the voices were still behind. He still couldn't figure out how the Cubans knew they had come ashore.

He stopped abruptly. The Hornet!

Had they found the supersecret airplane? The thought was nearly defeating, as though all had been for nothing.

Forget it! he told himself. *Move! Keep moving!*

The sound of the sea could be heard; gentle rolling

waves, not the crashing storm surge of earlier that night.

The beach appeared, white and crystalline through the heavy fronds, and he stopped.

Lowering Farnsworth to the kneeling position, he whispered, "I'll recon the front. Sit tight."

"I'm not going anywhere, brother," Farnsworth replied softly.

Slipping to the edge of the tree line, Sacrette scanned the beach. An army patrol was sweeping from the west end. Turning to the east, he saw another patrol materialize from the eastern jungle tree line.

"Damn," he cursed. In that moment he felt the chilling reality feared by all men on the run.

"We're cut off."

The voices from the rear, the north, grew louder as the soldiers thrashed through the bush like African hunters, driving a lion toward a waiting ambush.

Whirling around, he froze!

His fists tightened into two balls. Every muscle in his body coiled to strike as he felt movement to the right, behind a heavy, frond-dripping palm.

Catlike, he crept to the tree, formed his hand into a karate knife edge, then spun around the tree, raising his hand to strike the soldier.

His hand flashed down in a deadly arc; his eyes locked on the target, and from inside, a voice shouted: *No!*

Somehow, through will, or strength, or sheer compassion, the hard edge of his killer blow stopped only inches from the target.

Staring wildly from the other side of his hand, Sacrette saw two brown, fright-filled eyes filling a fragile face.

The face of a young boy!

14

"FOLLOW ME. I KNOW WHERE WE CAN HIDE."

Cucho Clemente motioned with one hand; the other touched his lips, telling Sacrette to be quiet.

Not knowing why, Sacrette obeyed. Cucho went straight to where Farnsworth sat waiting.

"We must hurry. The soldiers are everywhere," the boy said in perfect English, which Sacrette found intriguing. But without question, his instincts told him to obey.

Farnsworth jumped at the second voice. "What's happening?" he asked.

"Quiet," Sacrette whispered. "I found us a guide."

"What?" Farnsworth whispered incredulously.

Sacrette ignored the question. "No time to explain. Especially since I don't understand myself."

Throwing his arm around Diamond's hips, Sacrette pulled the heavy sailor behind the scampering boy. The voices were growing closer, and when Sacrette was beginning to believe the boy was leading them toward a trap, the skinny kid stopped at a large tree.

At the base of the tree, large bushes, standing four feet high, surrounded the trunk.

Pulling at the bushes, Cucho stepped back, then motioned Sacrette inside.

"A cave," Sacrette whispered to Farnsworth.

Sacrette shoved Farnsworth through the opening, which was no bigger than a manhole cover. Inside, he could see the cave had been dug out by hand.

Outside, Cucho took a branch from the ground, backtracked ten meters, then returned to the cave, wiping away his tracks.

It reminded Sacrette of his first bear hunt in Montana, where he wiped the tracks to his tree stand after baiting a bear trap.

(An hour later he killed that bear. Now, in Cuba, he hoped the boy was as good as he had been that cold November morning.)

Seconds after jumping into the cave and pulling the heavy bushes over the entrance, the boy's cunning was put to the test.

Soldiers appeared through the thick branches, their green fatigues wrinkled and covered with black soot.

Breathing stopped inside the cave. Movement was zero, except for Sacrette, who leaned slightly, as his hand went to the pistol in the shoulder holster of his survival vest.

Another soldier appeared, speaking in a low, menacing voice.

Watching the ferret-faced soldier, Sacrette saw the epaulets on his jacket.

Four feet away, Colonel Raol Escobar turned slowly, scanning the treetops. He knew how to hide in the jungles; his years fighting the Batistas and his jungle experience in Angola had trained him well. He searched with a wondering eye; wondering where *he* might hide.

Nothing.

Motioning to a radio operator, Escobar took a microphone from the soldier's backpack.

"Concentrate the search for the boy to the west," said Escobar. "We have found no trace of Cucho Clemente on the east end of the cove."

Sacrette stiffened. The officer had said "the boy." *They weren't looking for Americans!*

Turning slowly to the youngster, he didn't know whether to kiss him . . . or tear the kid's eyes out!

Quietly they sat, watching each other, the kid and the fighter pilot. The boy appeared in good control, admired Sacrette. A lot of sand in his craw.

Gradually the search drifted to the west. After an hour of stony silence, Sacrette popped his head outside the opening. Through the treetops, the sun shone in broken, golden shafts, warming his face.

Sitting back down, he looked at the boy. Slowly his hand came up from his side, extended in friendship.

"*Gracias, amigo,*" Sacrette whispered. A large grin etched his swollen face. "*Cómo se llama?*"

Cucho took the hand. "*Mi llama, Enrique Alavarez Espinoza del Busto Clemente.*"

Sacrette looked at him for a moment. "That's a mouthful. What's your running name?"

Cucho looked confused. "*Qué?*"

"Your running name . . . what do people call you?"

"My friends call me 'Cucho.'" A broad grin flashed across his face.

Sacrette nodded. "Okay, Cucho." He pointed to Farnsworth. "This is Diamonds."

Cucho's eyes lit up. "Like a baseball diamond?"

Farnsworth grumped. "No. Like 'diamonds are a girl's best friend.' Like me."

Cucho didn't appear to understand.

Sacrette glanced at Diamonds. "Good to see your sense of humor is returning."

"Where are we?" the CPO snapped.

Looking around, Sacrette shrugged. "Good question." He looked at Cucho. "What is this, your private underground hiding place?"

Cucho nodded slowly. "My friends and I, we built this cave. It is our 'digout.'"

"Digout?" Now Sacrette didn't understand.

Cucho reached back into the cave, then pulled out a battered stick. "This is our baseball bat. Here is our baseball. We hide our equipment from the other children."

Sacrette looked at the coconuts and homemade bat. "I'll be damned, Diamonds. We're in a 'dugout.'" He looked at Cucho. "It's called a 'dugout.'"

The boy laughed. "Okay. Dugout."

Then Sacrette remembered something. "You said your 'friends'? Where are they?"

Cucho sagged; the smile was lost in a slack face. "*Muerto.* Dead."

Sacrette looked genuinely touched. "How did they die?"

Cucho shrugged. "Last night. The devil water."

Sacrette shifted to the boy. He thought about the soldiers. Why would they be chasing a kid? Led by a field-grade officer? A kid whose friends were dead. And what was devil water?

Carefully the pilot put his arm around the boy. "What is this devil water?"

Reaching again to the back of the small cave, Cucho's hand appeared with the metallic globe.

Sacrette took the globe. "Tell me what happened, son?"

For five minutes Cucho explained. Sacrette sat quiet. He listened to the story unfold. The blond man. The gunships. The grenade. The boys dying what Cucho described as a horrible death.

"I ran away . . . frightened. I returned later. I had to go back. When I got to the village, I saw soldiers. They were burning the village. They loaded the people onto trucks. They shot . . ."

His voice trailed off. He remembered Antonio. Kneeling in the jungle clearing. A shot rang out. Antonio's head pitched sideways, exploding in a wave of blue-gray brain matter.

The blood!

He remembered the *constabularia*. Trying to run. The bullets from a soldier's machine gun struck him in the back. The policeman was lifted off his feet, sailing forward on his toes.

Cucho could still see the toe tracks in the wet sand where the bullets' impact carried the dying man forward.

The villagers were last. The villagers were killed to the last person.

"Jesus!" Farnsworth whispered. "That's why it took them so long to come after us. They were busy killing their own people."

Sacrette's eyes fell on the globe. "What makes this damn thing worth the lives of nearly one hundred innocent people?"

"There's only one way to find out, Thunderbolt," Farnsworth said flatly.

"Yeah. Only one way," Sacrette replied.

Carefully the CAG unscrewed the globe until it fell away in two hemispheres. One section of the globe had a machined hole. The second section was sealed with a countersunk screw.

Using his dogtags, he turned the screw counter-clockwise. When it came apart, he carefully tapped the outside of the hemisphere, aiming the opened flat side into his hand.

A small, round vial fell lightly into his palm.

"The devil water," Cucho said without breathing.

Sacrette held the vial carefully to the thin light beaming into the cave.

"What is it, Thunder?" asked Farnsworth.

Taking a deep breath, Sacrette exhaled slowly. "It appears to be some kind of chemical liquid. Very heavy in nature."

"What kind of liquid?" Farnsworth tried to lean toward Sacrette.

Sacrette felt a chill streak along his spine, emptying into his groin. "From what Cucho has described . . . the type used in biological warfare."

15

Naval Weapons System Laboratory.
Panama City Navy Base. Florida. 1215.

IN HER SLIP AT THE NWSL PIER, THE SES-01 *GULF Raider* pulled pugnaciously at her moorings, giving Congressman Noah Beamon the impression the sleek "surface effect ship" was ready to fight.

As chairman of the House Ways and Means Committee, Beamon was inspecting another of the projects requiring taxpayers' dollars.

In this particular case, he liked what he had seen.

The *Raider* was one of four of the US Navy's newest entrants in the "very fast boat" classification. Her planform was constructed above a sixty-foot SWATH where her waterplane area twin hulls converted tons of captured injected air into a cushion between the hull and the ocean surface.

Her weaponry was awesome: twin radar-controlled 20mm cannons that could be fired manually or by remote control. Signal LIOD optronic fire-control systems fired sixteen automatic tracking surface-to-air RBS-70 missiles; Swedish target-seeking TP 431 torpedo "tin fish" provided further surface and submarine attack capability.

Supporting the ship's arsenal was a Bell Kiowa helicopter gunship equipped with miniguns and SRASM short-range air-to-surface missiles, giving the *Raider* an airborne attack force that could wear down any enemy until the attack craft arrived on the scene.

To Lt. Commander Quinton "Skipper" Turk, who stood at the controls, the *Raider* was the meanest bitch in the Gulf.

He gripped a pair of energizing throttles in each of his suntanned hands. One set controlled the lift system; the other controlled the propulsion system.

Turk called over his shoulder to the small congressional entourage standing behind him in the pilothouse. "Lift gets us off the surface; propulsion moves us along the carpet of air generated by the lift system."

Headphones draped from his close-cropped blond head, his green eyes shone with anticipation of the power he knew would momentarily thunder through his hands.

"Okay," he whispered, "let's show these gentlemen a new meaning for 'float like a butterfly . . . sting like a bee.'"

Turk eased the red throttles forward smoothly, releasing the pulsating fury of the two 1400shp Pratt and Whitney ST-76 gas turbines into three waiting forty-one-inch diameter centrifugal fans.

Beneath the planform the turbines released their energy against the water, where the trapped air in the hull released a slow, winding hiss, cracking the atmosphere with growing intensity until a loud, monotonous hum filled the air as the boat drifted off the surface, held there by a noisy cushion of air breathing between the twin hulls and the bubbling Gulf.

Behind Turk the excitement was growing with equal intensity. Congressman Beamon grinned his approval.

"This is very exciting, Commander Turk," Beamon called through the headphones.

Quint flashed a broad smile to Beamon. "Flying this boat is like making love . . . you know the best part is always yet to come!"

Beamon pointed to the open sea. "Show me what this little lady of yours can do."

Quint winked at Lt. Willis Cole, the chief pilot sitting at the engineer console. "Ready to rock 'n' roll, Skipper!"

Cole was short, with the muscular build of a bull, and was the best helicopter and airfoil pilot known to Turk. He was watching the lift system's two pressure gauges.

Turk increased the pressure on the red throttle.

"Pressure's coming up. She's almost primed!" Cole shouted over the roar that increased when the red throttle forced higher pressure into a vacuum beneath the planform. A devilish grin etched his sun-weathered face; his blue eyes twinkled.

Lt. j.g. Cody McEwen, the weapons systems officer, chimed in her encouragement. "Come on, baby. Show these hard-assed chauvinists what a woman can do in a man's world." Five feet tall and blonde, McEwen was one of very few women the Navy allowed in fighting vessels; on her belt hung an electronic transmitter, enabling her to track a target and fire all the weapons systems from any point on the boat.

Quinton eased the green throttle forward, releasing the mounting energy from twin 6,000shp Allison 570 KF gas turbines into the waiting Rocketdyne PJ-24 waterjet pumps in the port and starboard sidehulls.

Supercharged streams of power surged into the

water, spitting out a low, steady stream like the firetail of a comet.

The *Raider* shot like a rocket, gliding on the cushion of air while her speed built faster than anything ever seen on the surface of St. Andrews Bay.

"Unbelievable!" Beamon's voice praised over the thundering hiss, which gradually disappeared to a steady purr.

As the energy was released into the water, the pulsators shoved the boat along as though a balloon had been suddenly released, the boat's internal pressure seeking the lesser pressure of the outside atmosphere.

"Go baby! Go!" Cole roared from the console.

Turk felt invincible as he leaned the power out to cruise at ninety-five knots. He stepped back, motioning Beamon to the controls. "Congressman. The ship is yours to command."

Beamon steered southeast. "She reacts magnificently," he called over the purr. "Such power. Such grace."

"I'll match the *Raider* against any patrol boat in the world. 'Any day. Any way.' That's our motto. Our Navy builds nothing but the best. Or we don't build them at all."

Fifteen minutes later the craft entered the Tyndall AFB drone target range.

Taking the microphone, Turk contacted the Tyndall range officer. "SES *Gulf Raider* on station. Send us some traffic."

"Roger," the RO replied. "On the way."

Turning to Beamon, Turk spoke confidently, "We've arranged a little demonstration for you, Congressman."

Before Beamon could reply, a shout was heard.

"We've got multiple inbound targets!" Lt. McEwen was pointing at the computerized operations console. The console integrated weapons systems with the boat's navionics, NAVSAT, and communications system.

Quint leaned to the radar scope. Four blips burned against the green field, growing closer. "Battle stations."

Cole took command of the console. Cody flew through the starboard watertight door. She could be seen through the bulletproof glass removing the safety pins from the missile pods.

Then she moved to the forward cannons, checked the guns, and returned to the pilothouse.

Cody freed Cole from the console. He dashed out the port door, churning along the weatherdeck until he reached the Kiowa. Within seconds he was in the cockpit, where he fired the turboshaft engine and waited while the rotors built to lift-off revolution.

Quinton was at the wheel. When he saw Cody was ready, he ordered, "Initiate target lock-on and infrared ident."

Cody's fingers skimmed over the keyboard on the console. Within seconds the targets' course heading, coordinates, and surface speed were plotted. Through satellite surveillance provided by the *LaCrosse* satellite roaming ninety miles overhead, an image of the approaching vessel filled the console's television screen. "We've got two airborne targets. Two surface targets."

Quint spoke into the boom mike. "Willis?"

A crackle followed, then Cole's throaty voice responded, "Primed and ready to move on-station."

"Roger," replied Turk. "Give us a canopy."

Suddenly the air throbbed as the Kiowa lifted off the rear deck.

"Targets closing." Cody plotted the approach.

"Target lock-on. Arm and ready," Quint spoke while watching the advancing blips. "Cody . . . deploy sweeping cannon fire and one torpedo on the surface craft. Willis . . . you take the airborne targets. Shove two rockets down their throats!"

"Roger, Skipper," Cody replied, pressing buttons on the keyboard. Moments later she looked up. "Target selection complete."

"Roger." Cole's voice came over the intercom. "I've got lock-on with the other two."

"Range?" Quint asked; he was staring through his magnification binoculars. "I can't see them yet. But they're coming."

"Five nautical miles and closing," Cody replied.

Quint took a deep breath, then spit the words his crew waited to hear. "Fire!"

Cody pressed one button on the console: a tin fish torpedo shot from the sidehull tube.

She pressed a second button, and 20mm cannon fire erupted from the deck.

Beamon stepped quickly to the radar screen. The four blips were drawing closer.

From the sky overhead two distinct claps of thunder were heard. Forward of the ship two white streaks of smoke left a long contrail from the rocket pods of the Kiowa.

Seconds passed. Quint watched the radar scope. The blips burned brightly. He checked his watch. Then the screen.

The blips still burned.

Beamon was joined at the screen by one of his congressional aides, who pointed excitedly at the screen.

A victorious cheer erupted in the pilothouse.

The blips were gone.

Beamon clapped Quinton Turk. "Beautiful shoot-ing, son. Absolutely beautiful. I've never seen anything like this in my twenty years in Congress."

Turk started to speak when he was interrupted by Cody. "Skipper. We've got an urgent message from COMCINCLANTFLT."

Lt. Commander Turk read the message:

Lt. Commander Quinton Turk SES-01 *Gulf Raider* and Crew* Ordered to immediate deploy-ment to Battle Group Zulu Station* Jamaica* Re-spond*

A broad grin filled the young commander's face. Passing the message to Cody, he ordered, "Tell them we're en route. ETA twenty-hundred hours."

Cody flashed the message to the commander in chief of the Atlantic Fleet.

Wearing a concerned look, Congressman Beamon asked, "What's going on?"

Turk shrugged. "Somebody's in a world of hurt!"

16

1400.

PAINSTAKINGLY THEY TRAVELED, USING THE COVER of
the dense, verdant jungle for concealment. Past low,
overhanging limbs that could hide soldiers in ambush,
or jungle cats in deadly wait, the trio threaded their way
along the finger of land called French Soldier's Point.

"How long we been moving, Commander?" Farnsworth asked.

"About an hour," Sacrette lied. Checking his watch,
he could see they weren't making good time. Three miles
in three hours.

"Bullshit," Farnsworth replied. "I've got you
slowed down to a crawl."

"We'll make it, Chief." Sacrette was guiding Farnsworth by the elbow. The chief looked ready to fold; his
swollen eyes were aggravated by swarming gnats. Stumbling through the rugged jungle undergrowth had left
his arms shredded by vines; his flight suit was nothing but
tatters.

"You *have* to make it, God dammit. You're the only
one that can get this information through. If the Cubes
are manufacturing biological bacteria from a chemical
plant, our people need to know. Please. I'm begging

you. Cut me loose, Thunderbolt. I'll take my chances."

Sacrette pulled at Farnsworth's elbow. "Quit your bellowing. You sound like a recruit in his first week of boot camp."

Looking ahead, Sacrette saw Cucho appear. "That kid is like a jungle mouse," he breathed. Cucho would walk fifty meters ahead, check the trail, then double back. He had been doing this for three hours. Soaked with perspiration, Sacrette was amazed that the youngster had barely broken a sweat.

A smile was on Cucho's face as he approached. "One hundred meters. Then we'll be there." He turned and pointed to the east.

"Good," said Farnsworth, pulling from Sacrette's grip. "You go on ahead. Check the place out. I'll wait here."

Sacrette didn't argue. "You're right, Chief. I'll go in with the boy. Run a quick recon. We'll be out in a flash."

Farnsworth released a long sigh. "Man, I wish I had a cigar."

Hearing this, Cucho ducked into the undergrowth. Two minutes later he returned, carrying a heavy leaf.

Sacrette laughed. "You're getting your wish, Chief." He asked Cucho, "Where did you get that?"

"Tobacco leaves grow wild in Cuba. The jungle is filled with them."

Farnsworth's head tilted to one side, toward the boy. "Did you say 'tobacco'?"

Cucho knelt and tore off the stem of the leaf. Quickly he rolled the first two thirds of the cigar, then bent the ends toward the center, leaving one third of the leaf tip for a flap. Next he rolled the flap around the stalk, licked the tip, and wrapped the cigar tight.

"Here. Senor Diamonds. A cigar." He thrust his hand toward Farnsworth, who didn't need to see the cigar. He was drawn to the aroma like a male dog to a bitch in heat.

Sniffing the cigar, Farnsworth smiled for the first time since crashing in the Hornet. "Man. I must be in heaven, Thunderman. This is a for real Cuban cigar. Grown in Cuba. Picked in Cuba. Rolled in Cuba—by a Cuban! Not a Cuban cigar made from smuggled out seeds and grown in Haiti, like most Cuban cigars."

"You can't smoke that cigar, Chief," Sacrette warned. "The smell of the smoke might give your position away."

Farnsworth shook his head. "Who's going to smoke? I'm going to sit here and lick and smell. You go on ahead. Recon the place. I'll be alright."

Sacrette knew he had reached the point where Farnsworth would be too great a liability. *Courage is one thing*, he told himself. *As is loyalty*. However, to sneak into a heavily guarded chemical plant, recce the area, and withdraw safely required at the very least the ability to see.

Not to mention a helluva lot of luck.

After stashing Farnsworth off the trail, Sacrette took his Louisiana Lightning knife from his boot, cut several heavy fronds, and camouflaged Farnsworth beneath the foliage.

Cucho led Sacrette to the ridge where the boy had first seen the blond European. Looking down, Sacrette spotted a chain-linked fence threading its way along a deep ravine. A high chain-linked fence ran along the base of the ravine; ribbon wire strung to the top of the fence signaled its nasty warning. Beyond the fence, a swath of three-foot-high grass stretched thirty yards to a dirt road.

"How did you get in there, son?" Sacrette asked Cucho.

Cucho pointed to the fence. "There is a hole. But there are land bombs on the other side."

"Land mines."

"Yes. I followed the footprints of the European." Shaking his head, he said what Sacrette already suspected. "The tracks will have been washed out by the rain."

Sacrette thought a moment. Without speaking, he went to a tree, cut off several limbs, then cut the limbs into six-inch-long sticks. He stuck the sticks in a zippered leg pocket on his flight suit.

"What are those for?" Cucho asked.

"You'll see." Nodding at the fence, Sacrette told the boy, "Show me the spot where you went through the fence."

Following Cucho, Sacrette started down the steep incline toward the fence. Reaching the bottom, they low-crawled toward the spot where Cucho had seen the blond European leaving the restricted area.

They pushed the fence, and a flap opened toward the mine field.

"You stay here," Sacrette warned Cucho. "We've got to do this the old-fashioned way."

Crawling through the hole, Sacrette held his knife out to the front. Carefully he began probing the ground with the moly-vanadium steel blade.

The "old-fashioned" way was to shove the blade into the ground at a forty-five-degree angle, using the knife point as a probe. At that angle, the blade would not strike the detonator. This technique was taught to American pilots in the event that they were ever shot down, captured, and put in a POW camp.

As he stuck the knife in the ground, Sacrette realized he had never thought he'd use the technique to break *into* an enemy camp.

He probed an area a yard wide, a yard deep, then signaled Cucho to follow in his trail.

Ten minutes passed. Ten grueling, nerve-wracking minutes. He had cleared an area six feet from the edge of the fence. Nothing.

Finally . . .

The knife point stopped against something solid. Carefully he pulled the knife out, took one of the sticks from his pocket, and shoved the stick into the knife hole.

"We mark the mine with the stick. That way on the way out, we'll know where they're located."

Knowing a mine field is usually laid out in a variety of patterns, with the zigzag being the most popular, and least ingenious, he scanned to the left front. Carefully he began an angular probe.

The knife found purchase!

Quickly he marked the mine.

Probing to a right angle, five feet away, he found another.

Marking the mine, he rose slightly. The road was ten yards away.

Thirty minutes later, he saw the gravel of the road through a curtain of green grass.

He had one stick left.

"Let's go," Sacrette ordered.

Crossing the road, Cucho started along a trail worn by heavy travel. Thirty seconds later Sacrette heard a rustling off to his side.

Then a deep, husky voice ordered in Spanish, "Stop. Put your hands up!"

Sacrette stiffened. Turning slowly, he saw the heavy jungle foliage along the trail separate. The surly face of a Cuban soldier appeared. He approached cautiously, pulling up his trousers with one hand; in the other, he held an AK-47 assault rifle.

"The bastard was taking a crap." Sacrette cursed his ill luck.

Cucho automatically threw up his hands. Sacrette shifted sideways, to a right angle on the soldier, who was motioning his rifle down the trail.

"What can we do?" Cucho asked nervously.

"Get in front of me," Sacrette breathed heavily.

"*Silencio*," the soldier barked hatefully.

With nothing to lose, Sacrette made his move.

Stepping forward, as though to obey, Sacrette feinted a step, bent at the waist, shifting his weight onto his left leg. In the same instance his right foot fired straight back, striking the guard in the groin.

As the Cuban went down, Sacrette whirled, executing a backspin kick. A sharp *crack* issued from the soldier's temple as Sacrette's heel found its mark.

Pouncing on the soldier, Sacrette saw the Cuban's eyes roll back as his powerful hands clamped onto the man's throat. He drove his thumbs into the trachea, his fingers shutting off the carotid artery.

A sickening, gurgling growl filtered from the soldier's throat; spittle pooled at the corner of his mouth.

Holding the death grip, Sacrette felt the pulse of the dying man running into his hands. Suddenly the cartilage collapsed around the trachea. A rush of air flowed from the soldier's mouth, washing Sacrette's face with a wave of nauseating, dying breath.

As the soldier plunged into a death throe, his sphincter released, voiding his bowels.

Die! You son of a bitch!

Riding on top, Sacrette smelled the waste, felt the soldier's legs jerk wildly, forcing Sacrette to squeeze with all his strength.

The death grip held firm.

Two minutes after Sacrette's foot found the soldier's temple, the Cuban twitched. Staring through bulging eyes toward the treetops above Sacrette's head, the Cuban noticed a slight movement.

Sitting on a branch, a multicolored French soldier finch joined eyes with the dying soldier.

As his mind began to snap, the soldier saw the bird turn to a blur, then disappear altogether as a cold vacuum pulled him helplessly toward eternal darkness.

17

1545.

LA CASA DEL DIABLO WAS SINISTER IN APPEARANCE. Not built into the ground, the complex shot upward through the jungle floor; it was as though some evil hand had pushed the buildings up from the bowels of the earth.

Two barbed-wire fences captured a mine field in a broken course around the facility, which was no more than a half mile in diameter. Armed guards walked patrol on both sides. There was one main gate, where more armed guards stood with vicious attack dogs.

Twenty feet above the complex, tall poles supported a network of camouflage netting, enveloping the entire grounds beneath a canopy that obscured a world within a world.

On the far side of the camp, a Hind Mil-24 helicopter gunship sat beneath the camouflage netting. Above the heavy rotors, a circular porthole could be quickly opened, allowing a momentary window through which the gunship could enter or depa .

The few buildings were Quonset huts built into the ground; their long hemispherical roofs were neatly concealed with cut foliage except where steps led down to doors at opposing ends.

"They must be troop barracks," Sacrette whispered to Cucho.

Sacrette and the boy sat high up in a towering eucalyptus tree twenty yards from the entrance, where the gravel road ended abruptly in a canopied parking lot outside the main gate.

From this position, concealed by the thick branches where Cucho had hidden while listening to the baseball game, Sacrette had a bird's-eye view of the facility.

Especially the one building that stood prominent within the Quonsets, a concrete bunker painted in camouflage.

Measuring two hundred feet long by approximately one hundred wide, the building was void of windows. On its roof was an elaborate exhaust system, surrounded by radio antennae stretching toward the gray, shadowy atmosphere beneath the canopy.

Of particular interest to Sacrette was the building's additional security.

A fence, topped with razor-sharp ribbon wire, encircled the building. Three more soldiers were posted inside the barrier.

Sacrette breathed deeply. A thick, acrid miasma stung his nostrils, erasing all doubt about what the Cubans were concealing.

"It's a chemical plant. The concrete bunker must be the production and research center. No wonder SR-71 and satellite surveillance couldn't spot the facility from the air. The plant is nearly invisible from the ground," Sacrette whispered to Cucho.

From his perch on a high limb, Cucho pointed at the main gate. He started to speak, but stiffened as the whine of an approaching jeep broke the silence along the gravel road.

Watching the gravel road beneath the eucalyptus, Sacrette held his breath as the jeep rolled into view.

"The *comandante*," Cucho whispered to Sacrette. "The officer from the village. The evil one."

Sacrette's eyes narrowed on the wiry figure. He, too, remembered the man. "He was the officer leading the search. I saw him when we were hiding in your dugout."

Followed by a tall, light-skinned man, the officer walked past the guards at the main gate. Moments later they disappeared through an entrance in the rectangular concrete building.

Taking a pen from his flight suit, Sacrette carefully opened a WAC flight chart of Cuba. Quickly he sketched the layout of the complex.

When finished, he motioned to the ground. "Come on. Let's get back to Diamonds."

Reaching the gravel road, Sacrette stopped abruptly. Motioning Cucho across the road, toward the opening in the fence, he turned and went back into the jungle.

Sacrette went straight to where the dead Cuban soldier lay covered by the jungle. Stripping the man's clothes and boots, he rolled the fatigue uniform into a ball, tied his bootlaces together, and then he draped the boots around his neck and picked up the AK-47 assault rifle and webbed harness.

Hiding in the tall grass, Cucho waited until he saw Sacrette emerge from the jungle.

"Let's go," Sacrette ordered.

Like a mole, Cucho slipped through the mine field, carefully avoiding the deadly mines marked by the sticks.

As he passed the last stick marking the mine nearest the fence, Sacrette paused. He took his knife, then carefully dug around the base of the mine.

Rivulets of perspiration streamed down his face, burning his eyes, but he dared not wipe away the sweat, as the mine gradually took shape in the carefully scooped hole.

"PRC 69," he said softly, recognizing the Chinese-made land mine that was the size and shape of a soda pop can.

The plunger rose menacingly, a death button for Sacrette should he jar the device.

Suddenly he had an idea. Crawling to the fence, he used his knife to snap off a piece of thin wire fastening the link fence to the support pole.

Carefully he straightened the wire, then ran the homemade safety pin through the eyelet at the base of the plunger.

If you bent the pin down at both ends, the mine was no longer a threat.

Removing the disarmed land mine, Sacrette filled the hole with dirt, then slipped through the fence.

Minutes later Sacrette and Cucho moved like shadows up the ridge overlooking the ravine, toward French Soldier's Point.

18

FARNSWORTH'S HEAD JERKED TO THE SIDE. THE bushes covering his body moved, then disappeared through his swollen eyes, which by now had become two narrow slits.

Slits through which the vague outline of two figures was barely distinguishable.

Pointing the cigar at the taller shadow, he leaned back, grinning broadly. "Hey, sailor. You got a match?"

Sacrette knelt by the CPO. "Yeah. Superman."

"Superfool." Farnsworth's voice was soft, mellow. "You should have kept boogeying straight for Guantánamo."

Sacrette said nothing. He recognized the sound of gratitude in Farnsworth's voice.

"We're on our way."

"What?" Farnsworth's stunned reply didn't surprise Sacrette.

"You heard me, Chief. We're going to Gitmo. It's our only chance. The hurricane has apparently changed course. The Cubes will be watching the gulf."

"What about the kid?"

"He's going with us. I can't leave him. Not after

what he's done. They'll strip the hide off him if they catch him." Sacrette leaned toward Farnsworth's face. "How are your eyes?"

Farnsworth exhaled slowly. "They feel like somebody's been standing in them."

"Can you see?"

"Barely."

"Barely is better than nothing. You'll make it."

"What's the plan?"

"It's not much."

" 'Not much' is better than nothing. Let's hear what you've got in mind."

Sacrette explained his plan.

A long silence followed. Farnsworth looked doubtful as he pulled himself to his feet. "Like you said, it ain't much."

"Yeah." Sacrette chuckled. "But it's all we've got."

Sticking the cigar in his mouth, Farnsworth asked, "What's our first move?"

Sacrette handed the dead Cuban soldier's clothes to Farnsworth. "Put this uniform on. It looks like it'll fit you."

Farnsworth looked warily at the Cuban uniform. He knew he didn't have to ask the fate of the original owner. "Damn. You mean I've got to wear a dead man's clothes?"

Sacrette nodded. "They're too big for me."

Farnsworth dressed in the soldier's uniform, adjusted the harness, then picked up the AK-47. "What next?"

"How's your Spanish?" Sacrette asked.

"Good enough to talk to the ladies in Spanish Harlem. Whether it's good enough for Cuba, I don't know."

Sacrette started down the trail. "Let's find out."

19

STANDING IN THE HIGH-INTENSITY FLOODLIGHTS beaming from the "island" of the carrier, Lt. Commander Quinton Turk watched Cody McEwen direct the assembly of the *Gulf Raider* on the fantail of the USS *Valiant*.

"That's an impressive-looking fighting craft, Mr. Turk."

The SES skipper turned to see Captain Lord approaching. Turk saluted.

"Thank you, sir. She comes neatly wrapped and packaged for travel. We can break her down into three sections, pack her into transport cartons, then load her aboard a Hercules C-130. The entire process takes about three hours."

"What about assembly?" Lord could see the *Raider*'s planform was being positioned onto the assembled hull by a crane.

"About the same amount of time. Three hours, give or take a half hour."

Lord checked his watch. "You can have that craft assembled by zero-one-hundred?" Surprise registered in his voice.

Turk grinned proudly. "She'll be seaborne ready by zero-one-hundred."

Lord nodded approvingly. "In that case, you need to be briefed." Without a word, Lord walked off, followed by Turk.

Reaching the ready room, the officers were greeted by the flight personnel of VFA-101.

Domino stood at attention in the front row, watching Captain Lord as he stepped to the podium. Lt. Commander Turk stood off to the side.

Sweeping his arm toward Turk, Captain Lord made a brief introduction. "Gentlemen, this is Lt. Commander Turk. Commander Turk is the skipper of one of the Navy's modern 'surface effect ships.' You may know the craft by the more familiar name of hydrofoil. Or PT boat."

"The skinny has it you've got a delightful-looking exec, Commander," Blade piped in. "I wish our exec was as pretty as yours."

Laughter rolled through the seated pilots. Cody McEwen's presence had swept through the *Valiant* within minutes after she came aboard.

Quieting the men with a wave of his hand, Lord began the briefing. Stepping to a television screen depicting the satellite transmission of the Blue Wall of Reina, Captain Lord placed the tip of a pointer over the dark image reflecting from the blue hole.

"As you gentlemen may know, we've located Commander Sacrette's aircraft. Our best estimate indicates that the Hornet is sitting intact in approximately one hundred and fifty feet of water. Our mission is to recover that aircraft."

A low whistle released from one of the pilots.

"That's some pretty deep water, sir. Not to mention the fact that the aircraft is sitting smack in the middle of the Cubans. How do you propose to make the recovery?" Domino asked.

Lord smiled. "Very quietly, Commander Dominolli. Very quietly. And very quickly."

Suddenly Lord was interrupted by a commotion coming from the opening of the ready room door. Automatically, all eyes shifted to the rear of the room. A marine guard stepped through the door, motioning eight men to enter.

Leading the group was a tall, wiry black officer wearing a US Naval Academy class ring and the insignia of a Marine Corps lieutenant.

On their uniform blouses, each man wore the gold badge of the Marine SEALs, gold parachute wings, and silver diving helmet—the symbol of the Navy's elite *U*nderwater *D*emolition *T*eam, UDT.

The men seated themselves in the rear of the room as Captain Lord continued.

"Gentlemen, we will be using an additional element on the recovery operation." Nodding at the new arrivals, Lord told the pilots, "Elements of UDT-One will conduct the underwater recovery operation while the SES attack boat will be responsible for covert surface security and the extracting of the aircraft. VFA-101 will be stationed at Alert Five status, ready to provide a TAC CAP should the Cubans intervene."

"How will the UDT personnel insert?" Blade found himself staring at the black marine. A sense of familiarity tugged at his memory. He knew the man; yet they had never met.

Lord pointed at the black marine. "Would you brief

these gentlemen on the insert...Lieutenant Farnsworth."

A sudden hush fell over the ready room.

"Farnsworth?" Domino turned so quickly he nearly snapped his neck. A quick study of the black officer brought a wide smile to the exec's face.

"I'll be damned. It's Daniel. Diamonds's youngest son."

PART TWO: ███████ THE SHINING PATH

20

COLONEL RAOL ESCOBAR STOOD IN THE BLUE LIGHT of Campo Viramo; his face was pinched into an angry scowl. In front of him, two soldiers held a stretcher. Lying on the stretcher was the stripped body of one of his soldiers.

"Where did you find him?" Escobar snapped.

One of the soldiers threw his head over his shoulder, toward the jungle. "Near the road. In the jungle."

Escobar thought for a moment. Then he looked at the body. "No wounds."

One of the soldiers pointed at the dead man's throat. "He has been strangled."

Escobar started for his jeep. "Take me to where you found the body."

Five minutes later the jeep pulled off the gravel road near where the body was discovered. Walking into the jungle behind the soldier who found the body, Escobar watched the soldier stop. Pointing, he told Escobar, "He was lying there."

Escobar flashed his flashlight into the brush. Pressed-down weeds outlined where the body had lain.

Escobar stared at the impression. Then he swept

the flashlight along the trail several meters. The ground was scruffed up in the center of the trail.

"They fought here." Escobar thought aloud.

He walked a few paces, then stopped abruptly. Kneeling, he flashed the beam onto something strange.

His eyes narrowed on the clear impression of a boot-print.

Running his fingers over the bootprint, he suddenly jerked upright. "That bootprint is not the bootprint from a Cuban soldier. It is a bootprint from an American boot."

"How can you say that?" asked Dorffman.

"Look. The pattern of the soles. I saw these same patterns in Nicaragua. They were worn by Contradoras."

Dorffman looked concerned. "The American plane that crashed last night. The pilots have not been found."

Escobar nodded. "They have now."

"Mein Gott!" Dorffman gasped.

Escobar looked at Dorffman. The scientist's hand was extended up the trail. Pointing to another footprint.

Escobar ran to the footprint. Kneeling, he ran his fingers over the smooth impression.

The impression of a bare foot. A child-size foot.

The apoplectic Dorffman gurgled what Escobar already knew.

"The American pilots. They are with the boy!"

21

THE FISHING VILLAGE OF SANTA ROSA LAY SMOLDER-
ing in a blanket of gray-white ash; wafts of smoke rose,
then flattened, painting dancing, ghostly images above the
charred ground.

A sprinkling of soldiers walked aimlessly about, their
faces coated with a mixture of sweat and soot. They
appeared tired, haggard; they had the look of men who
would rather be somewhere else.

Two hundred yards away, three figures lay concealed in the dense jungle at the edge of the only road
leading into Santa Rosa.

"I count seven soldiers. Six in the village. One on
the pier. They've got a jeep with a radio antenna," Sacrette whispered to Farnsworth. Cucho lay beside Sacrette, staring incredulously at what remained of his
village.

A chill rippled through the boy as he remembered
Antonio. And the *constabularia*. Trying not to think of
the horror, his eyes followed a course leading from the
soldiers grouped by the edge of the village to the pier
at the shoreline.

"There are the fishing boats." Cucho pointed at a

sprinkling of fishing vessels moored to the pier.

Sacrette scanned the pier. Most were shallow draft boats, sail-rigged. One appeared larger than the others, an open-water fishing vessel.

A single soldier walked patrol along the wooden pier near a gasoline pump.

Checking his watch, Sacrette turned to Farnsworth. "Give me thirty minutes to get in position. Then make your move."

Farnsworth shrugged. A coldness beamed from his eyes, which were now opening wider as the swelling in his face began to fade.

Looking at Cucho, Sacrette put his arm around the boy's shoulders. "You ready, Cucho?"

Cucho released a deep sigh. "I'm ready, Thunderbolt."

Sacrette patted the boy on the shoulder, then slid away; moments later his silhouette disappeared into the blackness beyond the road.

Farnsworth removed the magazine from the AK-47. Carefully he removed the bullets, counting as he reinserted the deadly projectiles into the metallic box.

"Twenty-six," he said softly to Cucho. He slipped the magazine into the weapon, then cycled the ejecting rod, loading the assault rifle.

Checking his watch, Farnsworth glanced to the moon. The moon was full, adding to the threat of exposure. "I sure hope Thunderbolt keeps his head down. This is our only chance, little buddy."

Threading his way through the jungle east of the village, Sacrette paused as he heard the waves rolling onto the beach. Slipping to the edge of the tree line, he peered through the bushes. The pier was to his right front.

Against the horizon, the image of a soldier's outline appeared.

Dropping to a crouch, Sacrette crawled from the jungle, slithering quietly toward the beach. At the water's edge, he pushed himself forward, then relaxed, allowing the retreating surf to pull him toward the sea.

The coolness of the water felt good against his body; the salty brine licked the cuts and scratches, burning his skin, yet bringing relief.

Thirty meters from the beach, he rolled forward, descending slightly beneath the surface, where he turned ninety degrees, beginning an underwater approach.

His tired arms pulled; his aching legs kicked, while the salt water burned his eyes. Watching the shallow bottom, he kept the pulling motion of the outgoing tide to his left, offsetting his body slightly to maintain a constant track toward the pier.

Surfacing quietly, he recharged his lungs with air, then rolled forward.

Three minutes later, the dark outline of a pole appeared. Then another, as the pilings of the pier came into view.

Gripping a piling, he relaxed, allowed his body to rise.

He floated underneath the pier, his lungs throbbing, demanding air; as he started to breathe, he heard the sound of heavy bootprints approaching.

Walking along the pier, a Cuban soldier stopped, lit a cigar, then continued his patrol.

After taking several breaths, Sacrette slipped to the edge of the pier. The soldier was turning, coming toward Sacrette.

Sacrette reached for the razor-sharp knife in his thigh pocket.

As the soldier passed, Sacrette reached up, gripped the Cuban's boot, and pulled with all his strength while thrusting his body backward.

Tumbling sideways, the soldier crashed through the surf. Weighted with heavy boots, grenades, and webbed harness, he began sinking.

Bubbles spilled from the stunned soldier's mouth; he started for the surface, but stopped as a shadow appeared.

Sacrette's arm snapped toward the soldier, whose bulging eyes followed the arc of the shiny blade.

The knife tore through the soldier's neck, severing his jugular, enveloping the Cuban in a pool of his own blood.

He tried to pull toward the surface. A hand gripped his neck. He tried to scream. Blood issued in red, exploding bubbles.

From above, Sacrette held the thrashing Cuban until he felt the body go limp.

Slowly the two figures drifted to the surface.

Pausing beneath the pier, Sacrette caught his breath, then released the dead Cuban as he pulled himself aboard a large fishing boat.

Feeling his way through the bridge, he reached the instrument panel. His fingers touched the ignition.

"Excellent," he whispered to himself at finding the keys in the boat's ignition.

As he started to inspect the boat, a shout rippled through the soft evening air. A shout he found both familiar and unsettling.

The shout of a man speaking Spanish.

Very poor Spanish!

22

"*Compañeros!* Come! Look! I have found the boy. Inform the *comandante*!"

Cucho Clemente walked in front of Farnsworth, his hands held high; his eyes wide with fear and uncertainty.

Fear brought on by the terrible Spanish spoken by Diamonds Farnsworth.

Farnsworth knew instantly that the situation had progressed from tense and precarious to piss poor.

"Get down!" he shouted as the soldiers started to unsling their rifles. As Cucho hit the dirt, he saw Farnsworth's arm motion toward the group of soldiers standing near the jeep.

From his fingers rolled a cylinder shaped like the soda pop cans Cucho had often seen floating in the sea.

The PRC 69 Chinese land mine floated end over end toward the soldiers, who were momentarily stunned by the unexpected appearance of the man and boy.

And the deadly device angling toward their position.

The mine struck the jeep, forcing the plunger into the detonator. A wicked explosion shook the night, sending a bright plume of fire snaking into the air.

Two soldiers were catapulted from the front of the

jeep, their clothes aflame, their bodies torn apart by flying shards of shrapnel.

A third soldier disintegrated in the driver's seat, where he had been listening to the baseball game broadcast from Havana over the shortwave.

A fourth soldier, heavy and surly, with a thick beard, was slammed to the ground. Rolling, the big man pulled at a pistol in his side holster.

"*Bastardo!*" Cucho spit angrily at seeing the man who had killed Antonio.

Raising his AK-47, Farnsworth unleashed a tongue of withering fire from the assault rifle. The stammering shook the air; a dozen bullets caught the Cuban in the chest, lifting him onto his knees, then back, where he slammed into the fiery ring of a burning tire.

Snapping to his left, Farnsworth met the challenge of another soldier who appeared from the opposite side of the jeep. With blood streaming from shrapnel wounds in his face, the Cuban ran straight at Farnsworth.

Straight into the molten river of bullets pouring from the CPO's assault rifle.

The Cuban's body seemed to quiver, then disappeared in fragments as his head and chest dissolved beneath the fury of the deadly fusillade.

"Diamonds!" Cucho shouted. He pointed to the right of Farnsworth.

Turning instinctively, Farnsworth sighted on the next soldier, who was rushing forward from the blackness beyond the burning jeep.

"Eat this, motherfucker!" Farnsworth shouted.

He pulled the trigger.

A hush filled the air as the empty weapon lay silent.

"Shit!" Farnsworth cursed. Charging forward, he

gripped the end of the barrel like a baseball bat.

"Get down!" a voice shouted commandingly over the din.

Farnsworth dove as the Cuban fired. The rush of the passing bullets popped like snapping twigs only inches above his head.

Looking up, Farnsworth saw the Cuban leer; he saw the rifle lower to his head. Then he saw the soldier stiffen as the sound of another weapon fired.

Crashing face down beside Farnsworth, the Cuban soldier lay still; his eyes stared emptily at the man who moments before had been caught square in his sights. A large, gaping hole above his eyebrows spewed blue-gray brain matter.

"He was going to kill you," the voice cried. "I had to kill him!"

Farnsworth rolled to his side. Cucho stood framed against the burning jeep.

In his small hands he gripped the pistol that had been used to kill Antonio Diaz and the *constabularia*.

23

SWEEPING CUCHO UP AS HE CHARGED PAST, FARNS-worth ran head down toward the pier. The sky roared with the light of another explosion as the jeep's fuel tank ignited, momentarily illuminating the ground.

Farnsworth's eyes froze on an object, lying on the ground; he bent as he ran, the shockwaves slamming him in the back, nearly knocking him from his feet.

Stumbling, he grabbed the long, metallic RPG-7 rocket launcher with his free hand, caught his balance, then continued his bullish charge toward the dock.

Another roar filled the air.

Not from the rear; a gurgling roar from the front.

"He did it!" Farnsworth shouted into Cucho's ear. "Thunderbolt's got the boat fired up and waiting."

Hitting the pier, Farnsworth and the boy were suddenly cast in a brilliant wash of light.

"Kill the lights," Farnsworth shouted.

After identifying the approaching figures charging from the firefight, Sacrette doused the floodlights, returning the night to a thick, velvet blackness.

"Get the bow lines," Sacrette ordered as he began to smooth the throttles forward.

Farnsworth had barely freed the bowline from the piling when the boat snapped toward the sea.

"Hold on, we're going to Zone Five!" Sacrette shouted as he firewalled the throttles.

The twin engines thundered; rising up from the water, the bow obscured the horizon. A long, white rooster tail of seawater followed in their wake.

Working his way from the bow to the flying bridge, Farnsworth found Cucho hanging on to the starboard railing.

"Come on, sailor." He smiled at the boy, who appeared in a state of shock. Gently he pried Cucho's fingers free, then carried him to the flying bridge.

"Where to, Skipper!" Farnsworth shouted over the roar of the engines.

Sacrette started to reply. Before he could answer, an earsplitting cry echoed from Cucho.

"Soldados!"

Sacrette felt his stomach tighten. East of their bow, the lights of another boat winked red and blue as it rounded French Soldier's Point.

"God dammit. If we didn't have bad luck . . . we'd have no luck at all, Chief." Sacrette watched the Cuban patrol boat close on an angle.

"Maybe not," Farnsworth replied.

Sacrette watched Farnsworth disappear toward the bow. Seconds later he reappeared, holding his hand toward Sacrette.

His big hand gripped the RPG-7 rocket launcher.

"It's our only chance. Otherwise, it's a Cuban dungeon for the rest of our lives. I'd rather be dead."

Sacrette looked at Cucho. "What about the boy?"

A great sadness pinched Farnsworth's aching eyes

into a deeper pain. "He saved our lives, Thunderbolt. He deserves a chance at life."

Without another word, the hulking Farnsworth grabbed Cucho off the deck. In a quivering voice, he whispered softly, "Take care, kid."

Cucho started to protest; he felt his body rise above the big black man's head.

"No!" he shouted, but he was flying through the air.

He hit the water tumbling; recovering in the foamy wash, he saw the boat disappear in the moonlight.

Moments later he heard the throaty roar of the engines as the boat turned toward the lights racing from French Soldier's Point.

"Madre Dios," Cucho gasped. "They are attacking!"

24

CPO Diamonds Farnsworth had barely reached the bow when he felt the fishing boat surge forward, nearly knocking him from his feet.

"Off the port bow," Sacrette shouted.

Kneeling behind the bowsprit, Farnsworth released the safety mechanism of the 40mm rocket-propelled grenade launcher.

"Range . . . sixty meters. Closing," Sacrette called through the darkness.

Sighting on the point below the red and blue running lights of the Cuban patrol craft, Farnsworth knew there was only one way to take the boat.

Dead on!

That thought was met with the sudden staccato of machine-gun fire from the patrol craft.

"Hang on!" Sacrette shouted. A tornado of bullets ripped through the flying bridge; splinters of wood tore from the wood paneling. In an instant, the instruments were shattered.

"Get ready, Chief." Sacrette spun the steering wheel to the right.

Farnsworth hunkered into the bow. The protruding

rocket lay hidden from sight.

The boat swerved to starboard, appearing to head for open water.

The Cuban vessel turned, setting an angle of attack that traveled along a line intersecting with the fishing boat's bow.

"Twenty meters," Sacrette called from the eye of a furious storm of dancing bullets.

Farnsworth took a deep breath, then waited, knowing what would follow.

In the next instant Sacrette chopped the power, turned full left rudder, toward the approaching Cuban patrol boat.

Another wave of bullets shook the boat as Farnsworth felt the fishing vessel's bow plow into the sea.

"Your momma," shouted Farnsworth, rising from the bow. "Here's a Dr. Farnsworth 'slam dunk.'"

Farnsworth executed a 'slam dunk,' a sudden power change maneuver used by powerboat competitors to get the inside line while turning around a pylon in powerboat racing. Sacrette watched as the Cuban patrol craft shot past.

At the bow, the patrol craft was visible for only an instant.

It was all Farnsworth needed.

"Fire!" Sacrette shouted.

The sea above the Golfo de Guacanayabo flattened beneath the thunderous quake of the RPG's launch.

Four small fins mounted behind the sustainer motor deployed as the rocket left the tube; at five meters the round was armed, traveling at 117 meters per second. At eleven meters the sustainer motor ignited, accelerating the rocket to 294 meters per second.

At that precise moment the HE round struck the Cuban patrol boat square in the ass!

The horror of death danced on the surface of the gulf.

The night turned red; the smell of cordite, burning fuel, and scorched flesh robbed the atmosphere of its salty smell.

Rising out of the water, the patrol boat looked like a comet flipping crazily through the air, then crashing back to the sea. Another explosion followed; then a rushing, bubbling gurgle foamed from where the craft sank quickly to the bottom.

"Good shooting, Chief" was all Sacrette said. He watched the patrol craft for a moment, then eased the throttles forward.

Turning a wide circle, Farnsworth didn't ask where they were going. He knew instinctively.

The external running lights came on. A shaft of light shot forward from the bow.

Moments later a small pair of eyes danced in the wash of the light.

Farnsworth's powerful arm reached over the side, and his hand laced around Cucho's wrist.

Featherlike, the boy drifted upward on the strength of his friend.

Lowering Cucho to the deck, Farnsworth hugged the boy, then lifted him into his arms. Walking past bullet holes, blown windows, and the smell of acrid death, Farnsworth went into the flying bridge.

Standing in the moonlight, Sacrette grinned broadly.

"You came back," Cucho said tearfully.

"You bet your ass," Sacrette replied.

Farnsworth coughed back the emotion, then asked, "Where to, Skipper?"

Sacrette nodded to Cucho. "What do you say, Cucho?"

Automatically, as though he had waited all his life to say the words, Cucho replied, "Oakland, California. In the USA."

"Oakland!" Farnsworth laughed. "What's in Oakland?"

A devilish smile filled the boy's face.

"Jose Conseca!"

25

"FIND THEM!" ESCOBAR SHOUTED INTO HIS JEEP MIcrophone. Throwing the mike into the seat, he pulled Dorffman into the front seat and drove away from Santa Rosa.

"There is only one direction they could go," Escobar shouted over the howl of the wind that blasted through the open jeep as the colonel drove crazily through the night toward Campo Viramo.

"Where?" asked Dorffman.

"Guantánamo naval base. It's across the gulf. It's the closest place they will find Americans to help them."

"They have the vials!" Dorffman wailed. "If the Americans get the vials, they will cause a political fury."

"To hell with the political fury, you fool! If the Americans get their hands on the vials, Zarante will know we have jeopardized his operation. Castro may put us in prison . . . but Zarante will cut us up and feed us to the fish for not telling him the vials were stolen by the KGB agent!"

Dorffman gasped, remembering Zarante's visit to the facility. "My god. He saw the container. He knows there were two vials missing."

Escobar said nothing. He only thought of the Americans. And the boy.

And his life, which was rapidly diminishing in value.

26

Battle Group Zulu Station.
North of Jamaica. 0230.

HUGE PHOTOELECTRIC LAMPS BURNED FROM THE IS-
land of the USS *Valiant*, illuminating the carrier flight
deck, where hundreds of personnel moved about like
swarming ants.

Leaning against the coaming of the bridge, Captain
Lord sipped casually from a coffee mug while watching
the activity on the flight deck.

Four F/A-18B Hornets sat at Alert Five; the pilots
buckled in and ready to launch. From the catapult shut-
tles holding the fighters in launch tension, hissing steam
drifted upward, forming clouds of mist that quickly dis-
sipated against the cool early morning air.

Beside the *Gulf Raider*, now assembled on the fantail, Lt. Commander Quinton Turk watched a heavy
hook lower from a boom crane to the surface effect ship.
Cables ran from the bow and stern to an eyelet where
the hook was neatly inserted; a boatswain signaled the
crane operator with a wave of his hand.

Slowly "Tilly" the crane lifted the *Raider* off the
deck; seconds later the fighting boat disappeared into
the darkness beyond the port side of the flight deck.

Lt. Daniel Farnsworth stood beside Turk; checking his watch, he motioned to his UDT team assembled near where the *Raider* had stood moments before. "Saddle up, Chief."

CPO James Lovgren, a muscular sailor of medium height, reached for his rucksack. With a snap of his wrist, the heavy pack filled with explosives, ammunition, and other essentials jerked onto his back with startling ease.

"Let's move out. Form up at the brow," Lovgren barked to the six enlisted men sitting by their gear.

Sitting in the cockpit of his Strike/Fighter, Domino watched the UDT team double-time to the brow, now hanging in place over the port side of the carrier.

Reaching the brow, the men walked down the long steps leading to the surface of the Caribbean.

A loud whine broke the air; a pulsating throb shook the surface as the *Gulf Raider*'s engines came to life. In the pilothouse, Lt. Cole lightly shoved the throttles forward, easing the craft toward the brow.

"Load them up, Chief," Lt. Farnsworth ordered.

The UDT team stepped aboard the *Gulf Raider*, followed by Turk and Farnsworth.

On the weather deck, large coils of cable stood in neat rows; at the fantail, a heavy winch had been installed for the mission.

Dropping their gear near their twin-scuba rigs, the UDT men sat on the deck, surrounded by several DPVs. Each diver propulsion vehicle was saddled with a large pouch; inside the pouch rested the weapons and equipment they would use underwater once they reached the aircraft.

"I sure hope this works, sir." Lovgren pointed at the winch.

"It has to work," Daniel replied.

Lovgren didn't look convinced. "We're forty-five miles from the Jardines, Lieutenant. That's inside Cuban territorial water. Even using the cover of darkness it's risky. If they catch us out in the open . . . our asses will be hanging out all over the place."

Daniel turned to the chief. His diamond black eyes burned like banked coals. Professionalism kept him from mentioning his father, who was now somewhere inside Cuba. Confidence in his men, their equipment, and the necessity of the mission formulated his response.

"They won't catch us in the open. Our insert path will be covered by satellite jamming. The Cubans won't know we're there. Now get some rest. We've got a long morning ahead."

Lovgren shrugged, then squeezed Daniel's shoulder. He said what none of the other UDT team members had dared say since arriving aboard the carrier. "He's alright, sir. I know your old man. We served together in Nam. He can take care of himself better than any man I know."

Daniel nodded gratefully, then walked to the fantail. In the shadows beneath the massive carrier, he felt the *Raider* begin to drift to port.

In the pilothouse Quinton Turk stepped to the controls. Beads of sweat streaked his suntanned face, which glowed red from the instrument panel lights.

Speaking into the boom mike, Turk contacted the CIC. "*Gulf Raider* ready for deployment."

Hearing the contact, Captain Lord walked smartly to the CIC. Taking the microphone, he ordered, "*Gulf Raider* cleared for deployment. Good hunting, Commander Turk."

It was then, while waiting for Turk's reply, that the radar operator seated at a nearby console rose excitedly from his seat.

"Holy balls! We've got surface traffic, Captain. It looks like the whole Cuban navy is in the gulf!"

Lord darted to the radar console. "Damn!" he cursed.

Depicting the surface of the area near the Blue Wall of Reina, the radar screen was aglow with the steady burn of no less than twelve blips.

A thousand questions flashed through Lord's mind; questions that seemed to imply the same answer:

The Cubans knew the location of Sacrette's aircraft!

Taking the microphone, Lord issued his command in a voice hot with loathing.

"All elements of Operation Bold Forager stand down. We are at station X-Ray. Launch the Alert Five!"

27

"LAUNCH THE ALERT FIVE," THE VOICE OF THE AIR boss exploded over the 1-MC intercom on the flight deck.

Sitting in his cockpit, Lt. Darrel Blaisedale saluted the air boss, then gripped the HOTAS, anticipating what was about to happen. His aircraft was locked in the tension of Cat One, cocked like a crossbow.

Suddenly, as the catapult was fired, his F/A-18 Strike/Fighter shot along the cat track in a cloud of swirling steam.

Twenty transverse g's slammed his body deep into the seat; his vision was reduced to tunnel vision. Facial skin peeled back in a grotesque mask. His vocal cords hardened as though made of strands of steel, turning his voice into a low, guttural groan.

"Wolf Three . . . departing Home Plate."

Blade shoved the throttles through military power into Zone Five afterburner. He pulled back on the HOTAS, and in a heartbeat the Hornet was climbing through Angels twelve in a "pure vertical" afterburner climb.

Feeling his speed jeans tighten as the g-meter ticked through nine times the force of gravity, Blade summoned all his strength to turn his head to the port wing. Below the eerie image created by the condensation wafting from the wing root, he saw a streak of fire burn along the flight deck of the *Valiant*.

A split second later he shot through Angels eighteen as he heard Domino's voice call over the radio.

"Wolf Two . . . departing Home Plate."

Three minutes after the cat shot, Blade heard Domino check in.

"Wolf Three . . . this is Wolf Two. Have your six in my sights. Now pulling onto your three."

Glancing out the starboard side of the cockpit, Blade saw Domino's tandem-seat Hornet pull onto his right wing position.

Listening on the crypto frequency, Blade heard Domino contact Captain Lord in the CIC.

"Umpire, this is Wolf Two. Request instructions."

"Wolf Two . . . deploy to a position twelve miles west of Cayo Caballones. Remain on station until further orders. Have detected Cuban surface craft in vicinity of common interest."

Domino understood. "Common interest" was the code name for Sacrette's Strike/Fighter.

"What's the ROE?" Domino fired back to the CIC.

"Rules of engagement are as follows . . . Do not fire on surface craft without orders. Maintain rotation outside of international boundary at Angels twenty-four. If engaged by enemy aircraft, fire only if fired upon. Your 'bingo' is Guantánamo naval base."

Domino understood. The "bingo," or alternate field of landing, was the naval base on the southeastern tip of the island.

Before he could respond, the cockpit lit up with a

shrill sound from the radar system.

"We've got bogies!" Lt. j.g. Marvin Zak, running name "Caveman," shouted from his rear seat radar intercept officer's position.

Three blips appeared on the screen.

"Home Plate...Wolf Three. Have three bogies. Estimate nose to nose in thirty seconds...at the borderline." Domino spoke while mentally calculating the Cuban fighter plane's approach.

"Bearing zero-five-five. Looks like three of a kind ...MiG-27 'Floggers.'" Caveman switched on the weapons system.

On the HOTAS, Domino switched to another frequency. "Wolf Two...to Wolf Three. Have three inbound Flogger-class MiGs. Keep your eyes open, Blade. Don't fire unless fired upon."

"Roger. Wolf Two...locked and loaded."

In the cockpit Blade turned to his RIO, Lt. Carl "Axeman" Ackerman. "Get ready for ECM or full rock 'n' roll. We're going to get up close and personal. Very personal."

"Weapons armed," Axeman replied calmly.

The MiGs approached low, hugging the deck, in attack formation. At the two-mile point, the middle Flogger broke formation and shot straight toward the two Hornets.

"Inbound, and looking hostile," Domino called to Blade.

"No lock on," Blade replied. "They're feeling us out." The signal indicating their heat source had been locked on to by another radar source was silent.

"Got him on FLIR," Domino reported. Watching the forward-looking infrared radar projection on the

HUD, Domino saw the Flogger ease into his gun sights.

"Bang," he whispered, mentally squeezing the trigger.

The Flogger responded with his own devious game.

"He's on my twelve. Coming straight down my throat!" Blade shouted.

"Break off . . . break off!" Domino shouted.

"Fuck the bastard!" Blade replied. "I don't back off from a Cuban! He wants to play fast and loose. That's the Blademan's favorite game. Shut down the radar, Axeman. Let's see how good this sucker is in the dark!"

Shoving the nose forward, Blade took a direct line on the approaching Flogger.

Domino's voice filled Blade's cockpit as he shouted orders the younger pilot ignored.

Watching the duel approach critical mass, Domino sat helpless in his cockpit. From the FLIR scan, two images suddenly appeared on the HUD where a moment before there had been only one.

Blade was on the screen, flying at Mach two toward the approaching Flogger.

"Pull out, Blade. Pull out and get on my three. That's an order!"

For Blade, the line was drawn.

It led straight to the nose of the inbound MiG Flogger.

Both aircraft closed the distance faster than human reaction time could have allowed them to call off the duel.

The Flogger struck Blade's Hornet at the starboard wing root.

Instantly the Flogger exploded in a thunderclap of brilliant orange-red fire.

With one wing torn off, Blade's Hornet tumbled crazily through the sky, spinning the trapped aviators in their seats under the impact of more than a hundred g's.

The blood pooling in Blade's head brought on a "red-out"; consciousness drained before he knew the blood vessels in his brain had exploded.

In the rear seat, Axeman felt the vertebrae in his neck compress, pinching spinal nerves that left his arms useless.

He tried to reach for the ejection handle between his legs, but nothing moved, except his eyeballs, which twitched crazily as the moon darted across the sky, disappeared, darted again, and finally was gone when the aircraft stopped its forward tumble.

When the full force of the Hornet's forward momentum bled off, the aircraft began a sickening downward spiral.

The left wing disintegrated, shredded at the fuselage. Nosing forward, the Hornet went to a full tilt vertical nosedive.

"Get out! Get out!" Domino's voice shouted over Axeman's radio.

Again Axeman tried futilely to reach the ejection handle. A low, pitiful moan echoed up from his stomach; a deep, seemingly endless cry for help.

It was the last sound ever uttered by the young aviator.

The Hornet hit the water in a sheltered bay offshore from Cayo Blanco at eight hundred miles an hour.

Two hundred yards from another pilot, who watched helplessly as one of his Strike/Fighters lit the black night above the moonlit bay for a fiery, agonizing moment.

Commander Boulton Sacrette.

28

CHARGING HEAD DOWN TOWARD THE CRASH SITE, Sacrette ignored the shouts from Farnsworth and Cucho, who stood at the stern of their disabled fishing boat.

The mothering instincts of the CAG drove him harder, powering him through the shallow water. Stripping off his clothes as he ran, Sacrette reached the downed Hornet as a final, furious explosion ripped the tiny bay.

Sacrette went down under the concussion of the blast; as he came up, the warm taste of blood filled his mouth. Blood streaming from a deep gash above his eye clouded his vision, but through the pain, the blood, he could see the cockpit of the Hornet.

On impact, the Hornet hit belly down, blowing off the clamshell canopy while launching parts of the fighter plane into every direction on the compass. What remained of the nose and cockpit section was buried in soft white sand up to the leading edge extension running from the wing roots to the base of the missing canopy.

As he neared the aircraft, he saw fuel burning on the surface; it cast a red-orange glow onto the tail section, which lay thirty yards away.

"No!" Sacrette shouted, recognizing the aircraft number he knew as well as his own *Double Nuts*.

Reaching the nose section, he stopped, staring at the cockpit; in the red glow two bodies slumped forward, still strapped to their ejection seats.

"Blade. Axeman." Sacrette's mouth tightened as he approached the remains of the aircraft.

Blade still gripped the HOTAS; prying the pilot's hands loose took all of Sacrette's strength.

Axeman's head was twisted at a peculiar left angle; unfastening the RIO's face mask, Sacrette gazed into his dead eyes.

Gently, almost reverently, the CAG pressed the quick release on Blade's torso harness. The harness held fast.

"Damn," Sacrette cursed. Taking his Louisiana Lightning knife, he cut the nylon straps securing Blade to the cockpit.

Reaching inside, he tried to lift the body out, but the weight was too great.

Suddenly a dark arm extended past his hands.

"Let me help, sir," Farnsworth whispered. He was standing behind Sacrette; tears streaked his face.

After pulling the bodies from the cockpit, Sacrette and Farnsworth carried the dead aviators to the boat near the beach.

Sacrette stood for a long moment in the shallow water, his eyes scanning the secluded island of Cayo Blanco, one of the many keys composing the Jardines de la Reina, the Garden of the Queen.

"Come on, Thunder. We've got to get our asses out of here. The Cubans will be searching the area in no time at all." Farnsworth was holding Axeman.

Sacrette glanced at the sky; stars twinkled against the black night. He remembered such a night, years ago, at Alert Five in the Persian Gulf. That was during the Iranian hostage rescue mission.

He remembered something else: The disgraceful way the Iranian government had displayed the Americans killed at Desert One. "I don't want their bodies found."

Farnsworth couldn't find an argument with the notion. It was the time element that bothered him. "What about the Cubans? This place could be swarming with the bastards any minute."

Sacrette shook his head. "This is an isolated part of the Jardines. I doubt they'll find the aircraft until morning. That's when they'll search this area with a fine-tooth comb."

Nearly stumbling beneath the weight of Blade's body, Sacrette walked toward the beach.

Three hundred yards inside the jungle, Sacrette stopped at a small clearing. Palms surrounded the opening; fronds dipped lightly beneath a gentle breeze.

"Strip off their flotation vests," Sacrette ordered Farnsworth. "And keep their pistols."

Farnsworth removed their pistols from the shoulder holsters of their survival vests. Next, he removed their flotation vests.

Using their hands, Sacrette and Farnsworth scooped out two shallow graves. Covering the bodies was the most difficult part.

As Sacrette shoved the loose sand over Blade's body, he remembered the young pilot's enthusiasm for life. His joy for flying. His soft Texas accent.

"Remember a few months back, Chief? When Blade and I flew recon through the Bekka Valley. He took a missile up his ass. Had to fly back to the carrier with the damn thing stuck in one of his engines."

"Yes, sir. That was a nervous morning." Farnsworth remembered that day off the coast of Lebanon.

Sacrette laughed lightly, a forlorn laugh. "He brought the plane in, right on the numbers."

Farnsworth shook his head proudly. "He was a helluva pilot, Thunderbolt."

With a final stroke, Sacrette's hands pushed sand over Blade's face, sealing the young pilot in his shallow tomb.

"Yeah . . . a helluva pilot."

Both men stood, saluted smartly, then said a silent prayer.

Sacrette looked around, then at Farnsworth. "Use that bearlike strength of yours. Tear off one of those palm fronds. I'll sweep our way out of here."

With the ease of tearing paper, Farnsworth ripped off a frond while Sacrette smoothed the sand over the graves, eliminating all signs of a grave site.

As they began retreating toward the beach, Farnsworth wiped away their tracks. Taking one last glance at the jungle clearing, he saw there was no sign of the graves.

Moving quickly, the two men hurried to the boat. Cucho was waiting, staring wide-eyed at the wreckage, a dark and forbidding presence in the bay.

Taking a rope from the boat, Sacrette started for the cockpit of the Hornet.

Following close behind, Farnsworth couldn't understand what was happening. "What are you doing?"

"Making the hunt a little tougher," Sacrette replied.

"How?"

"I want the Cubans to think Blade and Axeman ejected. At the same time, it'll cover our presence."

"I see what you mean. If they don't find the bodies . . . they won't know we buried them."

"Affirmative. I want them looking for two pilots. Not two bodies."

Farnsworth watched as the CAG reached into the front seat and pulled up on the yellow and black ejection seat arming handle marked SAFE.

"Easy, Thunderbolt. This baby is now armed and dangerous." Farnsworth's voice was barely a whisper.

"No problem, Chief. I could do this in my sleep," Sacrette replied confidently.

With the seat armed, Sacrette ran one end of the rope through the loop of the ejection handle mounted on the base of the ejection seat. Taking the end, he carefully backed away from the cockpit while the rope began threading through the handle.

"I sure hope this works," Farnsworth whispered.

"We're about to find out, Chief." Sacrette continued walking backward, playing the rope out as he walked.

Fifty yards from the Hornet, the two ends of the rope met in the palm of Sacrette's hand.

"Here we go. Pray the ejection launch system is intact," Sacrette said as he put tension on the rope.

Farnsworth shook his head. "I'm praying you let go of that rope in time. Otherwise, you're going to go for one hellacious ride."

Without another word, Sacrette jerked hard on the rope.

A sharp *crack* filled the air.

"It's working," Farnsworth shouted as the rocket

charges in the ejection seat ignited.

In the next instant, as Sacrette released the rope, the ejection seat separated from the cockpit.

A long, red comet tail streaked two hundred feet into the night, arcing toward the blackness of the sea.

They could hear the canopies deploy. Thirty seconds later they heard the seat splash into the water.

Sacrette nodded; a look of satisfaction was on his face. "The Cubes will think they ejected before impact. When they find the seat, they'll think they drowned, or made it to shore. In either case, they won't be looking for two men buried on the island. The bastards won't have Blade and Axeman to put on display the way the Iranians did to our boys who died at Desert One during the hostage rescue mission."

"What about the boat? When the Cubans find the aircraft, they'll find the boat. They'll be on us like white on rice." Farnsworth motioned to the fishing boat.

Sacrette thought for a moment. "Come on. I've got an idea."

Taking another rope from the bridge, Sacrette went to the bowsprit. Quickly he tied the rope to the fishing boat. Dropping into the shallow water, he began walking toward the gulf, pulling the boat in tow.

Farnsworth grabbed on to the rope, as did Cucho.

Thirty minutes later, the trio had swum the boat out into deep water.

"We'll scuttle her here. The water's deep enough."

Sacrette took an axe from the bridge, then opened the engine compartment.

The axehead rose, then fell, sinking deep into the hull. Two more swings brought a rush of water. Five more swings and water was rushing in from the sea.

Dropping the axe, Sacrette grabbed the survival vests. He took one vest and pistol for himself; the other set he gave to Farnsworth.

"One last item. Then we go for a swim."

Sacrette reached beneath the wheel. Carefully he removed the pack he'd stripped from the dead soldier at Casa del Diablo. Reaching inside, he removed the baseball-size sphere containing the glass vial.

After he put the sphere in one of the pouches on the flotation vest, he motioned toward the water.

"Let's get the hell out of here."

"I heard that," Farnsworth replied.

Farnsworth and Cucho hit the water together; Sacrette followed, carrying his gear.

Floating on their flotation vests, Sacrette and Farnsworth supported Cucho in the middle.

They swam southeast toward Cayo Caballones, the Key of the Giant Horses.

29

THE FRUSTRATION IN CAPTAIN ELROD LORD'S FACE
was shared by all the personnel assembled on the flight
deck. He stood in the shadow of the *Gulf Raider*, which
had been retrieved from the sea by "Tilly," speaking
slowly, his face etched with the fatigue that was shared
by all the men aboard the carrier.

And the one woman.

Lt. Cody McEwen handed Quinton Turk a Styro-
foam cup filled with steaming coffee.

"What's the word?" she asked Turk.

Turk shook his head. "It's been over two hours since
the aircraft went down."

"What about search and rescue?" She could see the
answer from his expression.

"Search and rescue was never initiated."

"Then they're either dead, or have been captured."
She spoke matter-of-factly.

Before Turk could respond, Captain Lord addressed
the personnel.

"We are temporarily standing down from Operation
Bold Forager." Captain Lord's voice was barely audible.
"As you know, the Alert Five crew was launched to

protect Commander Sacrette's Hornet. Apparently, his aircraft was not the object of the search vessels in the Gulf of Guacanayabo."

Domino sat on the deck, listening; still dressed in his flight suit and speed jeans, he felt like a one-legged man in an ass-kicking contest.

"What do you think the commotion was about, Captain?" Domino asked.

Lord clasped his hands behind his back and bent forward slightly, appearing to give the question some thought. He had been wondering the same thing since the surface craft had turned to a westerly heading, away from the wall of Reina.

"I'm not sure. But something had them on the move. Our people at Gitmo are trying to make a determination through their sources. However, we may never know."

"What about the recovery mission?" Lt. Daniel Farnsworth asked what they had all forgotten during the past two hours.

"The mission goes tomorrow night. We'll jump off at twenty-two hundred hours."

Lord started to walk away. Domino stood, asking, "What about Blade and Axeman?"

Lord paused, his face reflecting the pain of his next words. "We can't do anything for them."

Without another word, Lord walked into the island. Reaching the bridge, he went straight to the CIC.

Lt. Milt Floren was sitting at his console. Projected onto the screen was an infrared scan of a chain of islands.

"I've got something, Captain." Floren was grinning like a jackass eating briers.

"Show me," Lord ordered.

Nodding at the screen, Floren explained, "This island chain is the Jardines de la Reina—the Gardens of the Queen. A beautiful paradise of white sandy beaches. Turquoise water..."

"You sound like a tour guide," Lord snapped. "Get to the point."

Floren stiffened at the rebuke. He could see the captain was in no mood for generalizations. He wanted particulars.

"I plotted Lt. Blaisedale's last radar target." He tapped a spot near a long, thin island in the sea of infrared. "Wolf Three was over this island. Cayo Blanco. One of the few islands in the Reina's that's totally uninhabited."

Lord was growing impatient. "What do you have, Lt. Floren?"

"With the *LaCrosse* satellite, we can read the label off a pack of cigarettes from eighty miles up. But first we have to examine a general area to find a target."

"I'm aware of how *LaCrosse* functions, Lieutenant. Dammit. What have you found!"

Floren ran his fingers over the keyboard. "Scanning the area where Wolf Three went down, I spotted something peculiar. What do you make this out to be, sir?"

Floren's finger touched a dark image sitting in the red field.

Lord's nose nearly touched the screen. "Bring it in closer."

Floren pressed several more keys. The screen seemed to move toward the object.

Suddenly Lord stiffened. He touched what appeared to be two blades jutting out of the water.

"That's a moving tailplane of a Hornet. You've found Wolf Three."

"I found the tail section, which led me to search the area carefully."

Floren ran the photographic eye of *LaCrosse* down-range on Cayo Blanco.

Lord recognized the next image that appeared on the screen. "The cockpit."

"Do you notice anything unusual about the cockpit?" He pressed more buttons, and the cockpit appeared as clearly as if Lord was standing on the boarding ladder.

"Yes. The ejection seats have been fired." A strange look crossed Lord's face.

Floren took a deep breath. "Both overhead, and side-looking radar from *LaCrosse* confirmed that Wolf Three and his RIO did not eject. The ejection seat launching would have shown up on radar."

Lord thought for a moment. "The system fired on impact."

A big grin spread across Floren's face. Pressing more buttons, he said to Captain Lord, "Look in the cockpit. Lying on the deck."

The interior of the cockpit was magnified. As he scanned the cockpit, Lord's eyes suddenly narrowed on something peculiar and totally out of the ordinary.

"My God!" Lord breathed heavily.

He was staring at a shining piece of metal that lay in the floor of the fighter plane.

"Do you know what that is, sir?" asked Floren, who could barely control his excitement.

Lord smiled broadly. "I certainly do, Lieutenant Floren. That is a Louisiana Lightning."

Floren shook his head proudly. "There's only one man I know of in VFA-101 who carries a knife like that. Only one man."

"Commander Boulton Sacrette!"

30

FROM HIS VANTAGE POINT IN THE RIGHT SEAT OF THE Mil-24 gunship, Colonel Raol Escobar could see most of Cayo Blanco. The island stretched six miles long, one half mile wide at its broadest point; a barrier island in the chain known as the Gardens of the Queen.

To the east and west lay other islands in the chain; to the north lay Cuba. Hovering at three thousand feet, Escobar could see the faint outline of Jamaica on the southern horizon.

Below lay the remains of the American fighter plane. The Cuban MiG-27 Flogger was unrecoverable, lost to the deep in its watery crash in the open Caribbean.

Dozens of Cuban patrol boats sprinkled the surface; recovery of the American fighter had begun since its discovery shortly after sunrise. What would follow lay in the hands of the politicians; for now, Escobar had his own troubles.

He, too, had his own form of wreckage to recover. The sphere containing the chemical sample.

And the two men positively identified as Americans by a survivor from last night's attack at Santa Rosa. Faces had been seen. Voices heard.

One of the voices was a boy's.

Coincidence? Escobar shook his head instinctively at the thought.

What about the boy? Had he been working for the KGB agent?

Doubtful.

Mulling over the events, he knew one thing was certain: Zarante would roast him over a fire if the Americans learned of the chemical.

And he could hope for no mercy from Castro.

Castro would probably supply the matches.

Which brought him to the questions asked by the minister of defense regarding the deployment of surface craft after the attack at Santa Rosa.

Now, the army and navy were searching for the two Americans they suspected had bailed out in the Caribbean.

What if they found the *wrong* Americans and discovered the sample? He knew the answer.

Sitting beside him, Dorffman shared the same concern.

Perspiration streaked his upper lip; his eyes seemed to dart constantly from the surface to Escobar.

"This affair has become intolerable, Escobar. Your incompetence has put us both in great danger."

Silencing Dorffman with a beady stare, Escobar glanced to the flotilla of naval vessels dispatched to search for the downed pilots.

"You fool. You know nothing. The incident with the American plane has come at an opportune time. We can use the confusion of the hunt for the American pilots to cover our own search."

"Search? Search where? You have no idea where the

Americans could have gone. They have probably been picked up by an American submarine, or CIA fishing boat. Which means the Americans will know we are manufacturing biological warfare chemicals in Cuba."

"To hell with them learning we are manufacturing chemicals! They can't prove anything. But . . . Zarante! He is the most important reason not to let the sample become known outside our government."

Dorffman swallowed hard. There might be hope. "If we find the Americans with the samples . . . we might be able to keep Zarante from knowing the truth."

Escobar started to speak when the pilot shouted over the roar of the turbo-engines.

"Colonel Escobar. Down there." The pilot was pointing offshore.

Escobar's eyes narrowed on the dark outline of something lying beneath the surface. Motioning the helicopter down, Escobar raised his binoculars.

Drawing closer to the surface, the outline grew clearer in the turquoise water.

"A fishing boat!" Escobar slapped his leg triumphantly.

Dorffman leaned forward. "A fishing boat. Yes. But is it the fishing boat the Americans stole?"

The Mil-24 hovered a few feet above the surface; a veil of water rose in the updraft of the turning rotors, but through the mist Escobar could see what he had hoped to find.

"Look. The identification number. The number begins with the letters SR. SR. Santa Rosa. There was only one boat in Santa Rosa of this class."

Something else caught his eye on the sunken fishing boat.

As he pointed to the bow resting fifteen feet below the surface, Escobar watched Dorffman's eyes widen.

"Bullet holes!" the scientist exclaimed.

Escobar nodded. "They have been here."

"Perhaps they are on Cayo Grande." The thought sent a chill through Dorffman. If the Cuban navy had captured the Americans, they would join each other on the torture rack.

Taking the microphone, Escobar spoke quickly. The response from the Cuban officer commanding the search for the pilots brought a thin smile to the colonel's face.

"The navy found nothing on Cayo Grande."

"Then they have been picked up!" The scientist's worried look turned into a mask of despair.

Scanning west, then south, Escobar saw nothing. Instinctively, he knew the Americans had not been picked up. The incidents of earlier that morning would have foiled any pickup attempt.

Raising the binoculars, he looked to the southeast. The Gardens of the Queen stretched in radiant splendor.

Speaking quickly, Escobar gave a brisk order to the naval commander. "Conduct your search to the northwest, toward Cayo Cinco Balas. I will search to the southeast, toward Doce Leguas."

Playing a hunch, and knowing the current in that part of the Reina's, Escobar raised his arm, pointing the pilot onto the new course. "Fly southeast. To Cayo Caballones."

"What makes you think they went in that direction, Escobar? The wiser move would have been northwest. In the direction you sent the search vessels. There are more fishing villages in the northwest chain. They can steal a boat and make their escape."

Escobar held up a map of the island chains.

Dorffman studied the key they were approaching. Suddenly his eyebrows arched as he noted the symbol clearly marked on the south side of Cayo Caballones.

Dorffman breathed heavily. "They must be insane!"

31

0900.

LIKE A PERSISTENT TOOTHACHE, THE IMAGE OF THE knife tormented Captain Lord. Floren was right; only one pilot aboard the *Valiant* carried a Louisiana Lightning. The knife's name, Lightning, and Sacrette's running name, Thunderbolt, were too closely related.

It was the name similarity that had led the pilots of VFA-101 to present the knife to him the day he was promoted to CAG of the Fighting Hornets.

Another suspicion gnawed at the battle group commander.

If Sacrette had found the Hornet, and had fired the ejection system, there were only two possible reasons for his actions.

Blade and Axeman were dead. Or seriously injured.

In either event, he suspected Sacrette wanted the Cuban army to think the pilots had ejected. A very risky move on Sacrette's part; the hunt for the pilots could lead to the discovery of Sacrette and Farnsworth.

"What in the hell are you doing, Commander Sacrette?" Lord asked aloud in the privacy of his sea cabin.

An answer didn't come. What he heard was a firm rap at his cabin door.

Lord found Lieutenant Daniel Farnsworth standing at the door.

"You wanted to see me, sir?" Daniel asked.

Lord motioned the young officer into the sea cabin with a wave of his arm.

"We haven't had an opportunity to discuss your father. He's a good man, Lieutenant Farnsworth. One of the best I've ever known. I know this must be difficult for you."

Daniel's dark eyes seemed to sag momentarily; then a glow pushed away the sadness. "He's alive, sir. I know he's alive."

"There's a strong possibility you may be right." Lord was smiling.

Daniel's head snapped toward Lord. "Do you know something, sir?"

Lord revealed to the UDT leader the findings of the satellite scan of Cayo Grande. And the knife belonging to Commander Sacrette.

"I'm sure you realize their situation at this point," Lord added.

Daniel's mouth tightened, then relaxed as his father's predicament was clarified. "They're in the middle of the search area. They could be discovered accidentally."

"That's correct." Lord strode to his desk. Spread on the desktop was a detailed map of Cuba. Circled in red was the island chain of Jardines de la Reina.

Pointing to Cayo Grande, Lord's finger slid southeast, to the next island in the chain.

"If I were Commander Sacrette, this is where I would be heading."

Farnsworth looked at Lord's finger; it was tapping

a small cove on the south side of Cayo Caballones.

Daniel shook his head in amazement. "I'll be damned. Right under their noses."

Tapping the symbol sitting at the edge of the cove, Lord had to laugh at the absurdity of what he was thinking.

As did Daniel Farnsworth, who recognized the symbol denoting a Cuban air force base.

32

1200.

"THERE'S OUR TICKET." HIDING IN THE DENSE UN-
dergrowth at the edge of the jungle, Sacrette pointed at
a Hind Mil-24 gunship parked on the tarmac of the Cuban air force base. A twelve-foot-high fence encircled
the base; guards patrolled the perimeter of the airstrip
where the constant takeoff and landing of Soviet-built
aircraft shook the sky.

Looking up, Farnsworth could see four "Acrid" AA-
6 air-to-air missiles mounted on the underside wing py-
lons of an MiG-25 Foxbat flaring for landing.

"There's a shitload of activity, Thunderbolt. I don't
see how you expect to get near that Hind without getting
your ass shot off."

Sacrette grinned. "Style and panache, Chief. Style.
And panache. Along with a pinch of luck."

Farnsworth shook his head. "Pinch? A pound is what
we need."

Cucho squeezed Sacrette's arm. The groan of a vehicle signaled its approach. *"Soldados."*

Appearing on a winding, rut-filled trail carved along
the outside of the fence, the jeep slowed, then drew to
a halt.

Two soldiers and a civilian stepped out of the jeep.

"Damn," Sacrette cursed.

Farnsworth felt his stomach tighten. He sensed Sacrette knew the men.

"What's the matter, Thunderbolt?"

"It's the commander of the chemical plant. The bastard who's been chasing us for two days."

Standing at the rear of the jeep, Colonel Raol Escobar lit a cigar, then turned to the jungle.

Sacrette felt a strange sensation overtake his body. "Christ. He acts like he knows we're watching him."

Farnsworth released a long sigh. "He's got the nose of a bloodhound."

"Shark is a better name. He smells our blood."

Suddenly the trio stiffened.

"Don't move," Sacrette whispered.

The colonel's driver was walking toward them.

Unzipping his pants!

Time seemed to stand still as the driver stopped two feet from where they lay hidden.

The sound of urine drummed against a heavy leaf hanging over Farnsworth; then the acrid smell stung his nostrils. Lying helpless, he felt a humiliating warmth flood his body as the urine soaked the ground beneath his armpit.

The cocksucker's pissing in my ear!

Farnsworth's silent rage threatened to explode. The seconds turned into what seemed to become hours. Finally, the driver shook himself, stepped back, and released a long, howling fart.

Somewhere between shaking his dick and cutting the fart, the soldier had unknowingly unleashed the wrath of CPO Diamonds Farnsworth.

Farnsworth jerked upright from the jungle floor. His bearlike paws clamped onto the startled Cuban's throat.

"Fuck!" Sacrette growled. Snapping upright, he stared momentarily into the soldier's bulging eyes. Eyes that appeared ready to explode from their sockets.

Charging toward the jeep, Sacrette saw Escobar reach for the flap on his holster.

Ten meters!

Sacrette mentally measured the distance while closing the gap between the Cuban officer and himself.

Escobar's hand gripped a Star automatic pistol.

Five meters!

Sacrette saw the weapon coming out of the holster.

Thunderbolt left the ground with the suddenness of a striking snake. His right leg shot straight out, his left bent at the knee in a flying side kick.

Escobar felt his rib cage crumble beneath the weight of the blow as the American's heel caught him in the sternum.

A sharp, sickening *crack* echoed as Escobar's feet flew straight out; bent at the waist, the wiry Cuban rotated through the air.

Rolling to his feet, Sacrette spun onto the man dressed in civilian clothing.

Frozen by the suddenness of the attack, Dorffman stared wild-eyed at the attacking American.

"No!" Dorffman shouted. Spittle flew from his mouth.

Sacrette's hardened fist struck the scientist between the eyes, shattering the lenses of his glasses. Dorffman's eyes crossed, then rolled inward toward his brain.

Turning, Sacrette heard a low, throaty gurgle issue from the tree line. Farnsworth was still holding the driver by the throat; rage continued to boil from his diamond black eyes.

"You won't piss on anybody else, sucker," Farnsworth seethed. Releasing his grip, Farnsworth stepped back as the driver dropped in a heap.

"God dammit, Chief. What in the hell's the matter with you?" Sacrette approached Farnsworth, looking as though the CPO would be his next target.

Farnsworth sank to his knees, his self-control slowly returning. He picked up a small rock; slowly, he rolled the pebble between his palms.

"I've made us a clusterfuck, sir." Farnsworth shrugged like a child caught with his hands in the cookie jar.

"Clusterfuck? Disasterfuck is a better description." Sacrette looked back at Escobar. The DGI officer was lying on his side, holding his chest.

Dorffman lay spread-eagled nearby.

Without another word, Sacrette reached through the jungle foliage, swept his gear off the ground, and spoke sharply to Cucho. "Come on. We're getting out of here."

Farnsworth nodded to the two men lying near the jeep. "What about them?"

Sacrette reached down and pulled a long knife from a sheath on the dead driver's webbed belt. A coldness filled his eyes as he started to approach Escobar.

Watching Sacrette come near, Escobar weakly threw out his hand. His voice was more grunt than groan. "No! I can help you. I can help you."

Sacrette stopped. Casting Escobar a contemptuous look, he thought about Cucho's village. Then he thought about the situation.

Walking past Escobar, Sacrette picked up the officer's pistol. "How can you help? More importantly . . . why should you help?"

Escobar strained to talk. "You have the advantage, senor. And a sample of the chemical. If your government learns of the chemical plant, there will be repercussions."

Sacrette grinned. "Good old Fidel might paddle your ass, huh, amigo?"

Escobar shook his head. "No, senor. Castro is the least of my worries."

"The least? I should think you would be more worried about Castro. Who else is . . ." Sacrette stopped in the middle of his sentence.

Suddenly he grabbed Escobar by the throat. Putting the pistol to his throat, he said coldly, "Who the fuck are you making this shit for, Colonel?"

"If I tell you, you must give us assistance," Escobar pleaded.

Farnsworth whistled. "The son of a bitch is trying to cut a deal. Right on his home ground. He's got to be chin deep in some real shit."

Sacrette handed Farnsworth the pistol. "If he tries to run . . . shoot the bastard."

Squatting in front of Escobar, Sacrette told the Cuban officer, "Okay, buddy. Take it from the top. I want to know the whole story. Chapter and verse. Just what the hell have you bastards been up to?"

Staring at the pistol, Escobar rose to one knee. "My government has kept the chemical production plant a secret."

"That's a ten-cent answer to a five-dollar question. Any idiot would know you're trying to keep it a secret."

"Not even the Russians know about the plant," Escobar added quickly.

Sacrette looked at him curiously. "The Soviets don't know what you're doing at Casa del Diablo?"

Escobar was now on his knees. He appeared more confident. "No. But they are very suspicious."

Sacrette remembered Cucho telling him about the blond European. "You were penetrated. By the KGB."

Escobar glanced at Dorffman. "One of his research personnel was working for the KGB. He took the sample. We stopped him before he could reach a Soviet trawler waiting offshore."

"How could you keep something like this from the Soviets? Cuba is crawling with Russians."

"Not all of Cuba, senor. Our relationship with Russia deteriorates every day. Soon, we will be abandoned. Like Afghanistan. Angola. Our economy is in a shambles. The Soviets can no longer afford to carry our people on their backs. They, too, have economic problems."

"Why would they want to keep this from the Soviets, Thunderbolt?" Farnsworth looked confused.

"The United States and Russia are currently negotiating to eliminate the production of chemical weapons. If our people knew what Castro was doing, they would figure the Soviets were involved. Negotiations would end. We would start producing again. Which means the Soviets would have to spend more money on production. The Soviet Union's economy is flat on its back. Gorbachev wants to spend the money on industry and technology. Not on weapons."

"Then who the hell are they working for?" Farnsworth glared at Escobar.

Sacrette looked squarely into Escobar's eyes. "The ball's in your court. You tell us who you're making this stuff for, or I'll kill you. Now!"

Escobar's eyes widened as he said the name of one of the most feared organizations in the world. "La Sendero Luminoso."

"Holy fuck," Farnsworth said in a long breath.

"Sendero what?" asked Sacrette.

"'The Shining Path.'"

33

Sacrette mouthed the words softly. He, too, felt the chill sweep through his body.

"Jesus. Those are some murderous bastards," Farnsworth said.

"Yeah. Peruvian. I know a fellow flying in the Huallaga Valley, two hundred miles or so from Lima. He's an old Huey pilot from Nam. He's working with the DEA. They have Special Forces-like camps in the valley. Near Tingo Maria. Running ops on the Senderos. They are the biggest cartel outside of Colombia. And they live in a mountainous, balls-to-the-walls valley. And they're not afraid of anything. Or anybody."

Farnsworth rubbed his chin methodically. "Why do you suppose they want to get their hands on chemical weapons?"

Sacrette looked at Escobar. "That's a good question, senor. Why?"

Escobar opened up with all he knew about Zarante and his proposal to the Cuban government. "Joaquin Zarante, the head of Senderos, approached Castro. He wanted Castro to supply him with some biological agents to use against his enemies."

"Fuck me," said Farnsworth.

Sacrette grabbed Escobar. "You mean those crazy bastards are going to use killer bugs!"

Escobar nodded. "Yes. Zarante paid Castro to build a plant to manufacture the chemicals."

"Why Castro?" asked Farnsworth.

Sacrette answered for the Cuban. "The Senderos couldn't buy or manufacture something like this in their country. Or any other country. It would be impossible."

"I see. But if they had a country off the beaten path, with a bastard like Castro, who's already in the drug trafficking business, the shit could be manufactured in relative secrecy."

"Precisely," said Sacrette.

Farnsworth suddenly realized something frightening. "What do you think they were going to do with this shit? You don't just tell somebody you're going to use the bug on them. First, you show them you've got the bug."

Sacrette's mind reeled at the possibilities. "Zarante's got something planned. Something that could kill a lot of people. But . . . more importantly, he will use the bug as a weapon to keep the government off his ass. He'll let the US wage war against the Colombians, but not the Senderos. Not if they have something like killer bugs. They'll corner the world market on cocaine . . . and the US government will be too afraid to do anything for fear of reprisal."

"That defies imagination," Farnsworth said.

"It defies sanity, senor. Zarante is a crazy Incan. He has no soul," Escobar added.

"Neither do you, motherfucker," Farnsworth snapped.

Sacrette stood. "We've got to get this information to our government, Chief. By taking the two of them back, along with the sample, our people will have proof positive that the Cubans are producing chemical agents. They can then try to get to Zarante. It's the only way."

"So we're taking them with us?"

"Yes," Sacrette said.

Farnsworth grumped as he turned to Escobar, "I suppose you want to go to Oakland, too?"

Escobar didn't understand.

What Farnsworth didn't understand was how they were going to get to their government. "We're sitting here in Cuba. We're hauling around a kid. A Cuban officer. And a cold-cocked German. How the hell are we going to get off this rock?"

A slow grin spread across Sacrette's face. Pointing to Escobar, he replied, "The same way we got here."

34

1315.

IN THE READY ROOM, THE PILOTS NOT ON ALERT FIVE were lounging in small groups; conversation was mostly about flying.

It was their way of staying in touch with what they did best, while keeping their thoughts off the three empty chairs near the front row.

Looking at the chairs that hours before had belonged to Blade and Axeman, Domino wanted to think about the two aviators he knew were dead. Not Sacrette. Who could still be alive. He wanted to think about them the way he had thought about Lt. Juan "Munchy" Mendiola a few months earlier when the young RIO was killed by an Arab terrorist in the Mediterranean.

He wanted to think about Sacrette. Munchy was Sacrette's RIO. Both had ejected low over the water. Sacrette had survived. Munchy's body was never recovered.

That was the pain of this moment. The bodies of his men were unrecovered. And, he knew, somehow they never would be given a proper burial.

And Sacrette was missing. Was the CAG dead? Would all the responsibility shift to his shoulders? Permanently?

A strange feeling told him from the beginning that Sacrette was alive. The same feeling that told him Blade and Axeman were dead.

Slowly he looked at the walls. Red silhouettes of airplanes were painted on the walls. The "kill gallery" of VFA-101.

Libyan MiGs. Iranian F-4s. Even a Libyan boat Sacrette had sunk with a single missile in the Gulf of Sidra.

Draining his cup of coffee, Domino started to rise when he heard a voice over the 1-MC intercom.

"Lt. Commander Dominolli. Report to the bridge."

Domino made his way through the maze of narrow passageways, past the forward dining hall. Walking through the hangar deck, he saw the air wing aircraft, waiting to be called into action. Helicopters were kept in one section of the nearly three acres of storage area. Twenty of the forty-five F-18s composing the Strike/Fighter squadron were stored with their wings folded; the rest were parked on the flight deck.

The mood of the *Valiant* personnel was obvious; the men were anxious to begin the mission.

Reaching the bridge, Domino found Captain Lord sitting in his starboard chair.

"Let's take a walk, Domino," Lord said sharply.

Hearing Lord refer to him by his running name made Domino feel momentarily uneasy. Normally, the captain was a stickler for formality.

They went up to the "buzzard's perch," an open area above the island where off-duty personnel often assembled to watch the launches and landings. The sky was clear. A gentle breeze drifted in from the sea.

Lighting his briarwood pipe, Lord puffed methodically until a blue cloud of smoke drifted upward. Looking down at the flight deck, he saw hundreds of men in multicolored shirts standing at their stations, waiting to go into action.

In the distance the rugged outline of Cuba could be seen on the northern horizon.

Taking a folded piece of paper from his pocket, Lord handed the communiqué to Lt. Commander Dominolli.

The communiqué was from the Joint Chiefs. Reading quickly, Domino smiled broadly.

Extending his hand to Lord, Domino straightened to attention. "Congratulations, sir. Rather, I should say . . . Admiral Lord!"

The word "Admiral" rang in the air above the buzzard's perch.

Lord shook Domino's hand. "Thank you . . . Commander Dominolli." Lord's eyes twinkled as he spoke.

Domino said nothing. As he stared, wide-eyed, his lips formed the word he had just heard. "Commander?"

It was Lord's turn to smile. "That's correct. You've been promoted to the rank of Commander."

The joy quickly drained as Domino's face darkened. "Sir. I think it's premature to write off Commander Sacrette. He's alive. I know him. He's not dead."

Lord turned and looked toward Cuba. "I share those same sentiments, Commander. As a matter of fact, we have confirmation that Captain Sacrette is alive and coming in our direction. For whatever reason, he is not trying to reach Guantánamo."

"Captain Sacrette!" Domino blurted. "Thunderbolt's been promoted to captain!"

Lord was grinning from ear to ear. "Affirmative."

Domino shook his head. Then another thought sunk

in. "Good God. He'll be intolerable."

"No doubt. However, the rank does fit his station," Admiral Lord replied.

When the surprise of Sacrette's promotion wore off, Domino returned to Lord's earlier remark. "What makes you think he's not trying to reach Guantánamo?"

Lord explained the satellite observation of Blade's Hornet.

"Captain Sacrette found the aircraft, then disposed of the bodies. Afterward, he fired the ejection system to make the Cubans think they had gone down over water."

Domino tried to put himself in Sacrette's position. "Now he's making an end run. He's on one of those islands, looking for a way out. Which means he's going to need our help."

Lord shook his head, then raised the odds against Sacrette and Farnsworth getting off Cuba alive. "Negative. We can't do anything to jeopardize the recovery operation. The incident with Blade's aircraft has the Cuban government stirred into a frenzy. Fortunately, we dodged the bullet last night. The Cubans were apparently looking for Captain Sacrette and Chief Farnsworth. Not the submerged Hornet."

"You're saying they are on their own? That we're going to sit on our asses and do nothing?" Domino asked angrily.

Admiral Lord gave Commander Dominolli a cold stare. "Completely on their own until they're out of Cuban territorial water."

Domino said nothing.

Lord glanced at his watch. "I believe you're scheduled for Alert Five at fourteen-hundred?"

Domino nodded. "Yes, sir."

Lord said nothing else. Nor did Domino.

As Admiral Lord walked away, Domino looked out toward the sea. Somewhere in that direction was the CAG, who didn't know he had been promoted to captain.

A promotion Domino feared might be the shortest in the history of the United States Navy.

35

1345.

THIRTY MILES FROM THE DECK OF THE CARRIER USS
Valiant, the newly promoted Captain Boulton Sacrette
was unaware of his new status. Had he known, the promotion wouldn't have been given a moment's notice.

Dressed in the driver's fatigues, Sacrette rode in the
backseat of Escobar's jeep. Hidden beneath his folded
arm, the muzzle of the DGI officer's 9mm pistol was
aimed at the colonel's chest.

Escobar glanced nervously from the pistol to Dorffman, who sat in the front seat. Farnsworth was driving,
wearing the uniform of the Cuban soldier Sacrette had
killed at Casa del Diablo. Cucho sat beside Sacrette,
watching the main gate of the air base come into view.

"It's showtime," Farnsworth called over his shoulder while downshifting the gears.

A narrow, dusty road led to the sentry gate on the
air base; the noise of departing aircraft thundered overhead.

Sacrette leaned over to Escobar. "Chief Farnsworth
speaks fluent Spanish," he lied. "You say one word not
in the script . . . and I'll blow your chest away. *Com-
prende?*"

Farnsworth smiled evilly at Dorffman. Through clenched teeth, he gave the East German his final warning. "I would rather be dead than spend the rest of my life in some shithole Cuban dungeon. You make one wrong move, I'll tear your head off and piss in your lungs. Do you understand, Herr Dorffman?"

Dorffman nodded weakly. He looked like a man who wished he were somewhere else. The idea of being kidnapped was not amusing; the idea of the Americans escaping with proof of the chemical plant was life threatening. For his life.

The jeep rolled to a halt in a momentary cloud of settling dust. A tall, skinny soldier approached. His mustache was scraggly; his clothes loose and ill-fitting. He reminded Sacrette of a scarecrow.

"Good afternoon, Colonel." The soldier saluted. then stuck out his hand.

Escobar handed the soldier his credentials. After a quick perusal, the soldier returned the credentials and waved the jeep through.

Releasing a low sigh, Farnsworth eased off the clutch, then drove onto the air base. The road wound past wooden barracks badly in need of a coat of paint; soldiers walked aimlessly, looking more like field hands than military troops.

Sacrette saw a Cuban flag flying from above a white building. "That must be the H.Q."

Grinding past the headquarters building, Farnsworth glanced quickly at Dorffman. The German looked faint. "Hang tough, Herr Dorffman. In an hour you'll be sipping Cuba Libres. If you say all the right things to our intelligence officers."

Cucho said nothing. Pressing closer to Sacrette, the

boy watched another fence come into view. Beyond the fence, helicopters and MiG-21s warmed their engines on the tarmac.

"Business must be booming," Sacrette said to Escobar. "Why all the activity?"

Escobar's eyebrows arched. "The incident last night has Castro thinking the Americans are going to invade Cuba."

Sacrette laughed. "Why should we do that? All we have to do is wait for the Cuban people to bring down the government. It's happening everywhere in the Communist world. Poland. China. The whole glorious revolution is blowing up in your Marxist faces."

Escobar chose not to argue. Instead, he played his last card. "Perhaps. But there are more important matters to discuss."

Sacrette smirked. "Such as what, Colonel?"

"Such as you reconsidering this insane plan of yours. I will make you a deal. I will order my pilot to fly you to the naval base at Guantánamo. In exchange, you will give me the receptacle containing the chemical specimen. We will both have what we want."

Sacrette's voice took on a hard edge. "We've already got a deal. Remember? I spared your lives. Besides, there's no way you could let me and the chief get off this rock. We know too much. So does the kid. You have to kill all three of us. So sit back and enjoy the ride."

Escobar pointed to the distant MiL-24 on the tarmac. Four Cuban soldiers stood guarding the massive gunship. "I cannot control the situation once we reach the helicopter!"

"Be cool, colonel," Farnsworth ordered. "We're going to waltz through the door like we own that damn helicopter."

Escobar was beginning to look frantic. Gone was the clam demeanor. The professional control.

Dorffman was sweating profusely. A large lump swelled above his forehead, nearly closing his eyes.

As the jeep rolled to a stop twenty feet from the Hind Mil-24 gunship, Sacrette whispered an order to Escobar. "Get out. Dismiss the soldiers. Then get aboard the helo. Tell one of the soldiers to send for the pilot."

Escobar barked his orders. The soldiers started for the operations building sitting in the shadows beneath the control tower.

"Get aboard," Sacrette commanded.

Farnsworth grabbed Cucho and went through the opened side door. Dorffman followed, then came Escobar. Sacrette entered last.

The Hind Mil-24E cockpit is covered by two tandem blown canopies. Flat armor glass windscreens formed two protective bubbles around the cockpit, creating a cocoonlike interior. To the front, low into the forward fuselage, was the seat designated for the weapons systems officer. To the rear was the seat for the pilot. *The design is practical,* thought Sacrette. *A single hit couldn't take out both stations simultaneously.*

Climbing into the pilot's seat, Sacrette scanned the controls. Everything was labeled in Russian.

"Can you fly this bird, Thunderman?" asked Farnsworth.

Sacrette gripped the cyclic. "I'm the CAG. I can fly anything. The tricky part is the weapons system."

Farnsworth scanned the weapons station. He shook his head. "It's all Greek to me. What are we going to do if we need weapons?"

Sacrette looked toward the operations building. A

young Cuban flight officer was coming toward the Hind.

A grin stretched across Sacrette's face as he saw the solution to their problem.

Thirty seconds later Lieutenant Pedro Sisteros stepped through the side door, where he was greeted by the powerful grip of Chief Diamonds Farnsworth. Without a word, Diamonds shoved the startled young pilot into the forward weapons officer's seat.

Sacrette sat behind him, in the pilot's seat.

Sticking the pistol against the back of Sisteros's head, Sacrette asked, "Do you speak English?"

Figuring he knew the answer, Sacrette saw Sisteros's head bob up and down. "Good. Now here's the game plan. I'm going to fly this crate, and you're my RIO. My weapons officer. If we run into trouble, you're going to operate the weapons."

Sisteros looked at Sacrette incredulously. "You expect me to fire on my own countrymen?"

Sacrette grinned. "That will be your decision to make at the appropriate moment. It's what all combat pilots must face. You have to decide which is of greater importance . . . your ass. Or theirs!"

Without another word, Sacrette fired the twin Isotov TV-2 turboshafts. Slowly the four rotor blades churned to lift-off rpm as the turboshafts turned out over fifteen hundred horsepower.

Sacrette had scarcely started pulling back on the collective to lift the massive helo off the ground when a shout split the pulsating air.

"Stop!"

Looking back, Sacrette saw Farnsworth kneeling in the door. Beyond the door, on the ground, Sacrette could see Escobar dashing for his freedom.

"Christ!" Sacrette felt his stomach tighten.

He saw something else.

Gripped in Escobar's hand was the pouch containing the chemical agent!

FARNSWORTH'S CLENCHED FIST ARCED BACKWARD IN
a reverse punch, catching Dorffman on the swelled lump
between his eyes. Crumpling into a heap, the East German was no longer a concern. What ran ten feet ahead
of the helo was a concern.

"He's going for the ops building, Thunderbolt!"
Farnsworth shouted.

Sacrette shook his head while shouting. "Like hell
he is. Get ready to recover the pouch."

Lowering the nose into ground effect, Sacrette
shoved the throttles forward. Like a giant dragonfly, the
Hind raced along the tarmac in pursuit of the fleeing Escobar.

"Get ready!" Sacrette shouted.

Farnsworth leaned out the door; in that instant he
realized what Sacrette had planned for the DGI colonel.

Escobar could feel the heat from the thundering
Hind snaking up his legs; when his cap flew off from the
turboblast, his eyes widened as he realized what was
happening.

"No-o-o-o . . . !" The scream from Escobar was
drowned out by the noise of the hurtling Hind.

The leading edge of the first rotor caught Escobar on the right side of his body, severing his arm at the elbow. Through the blur he thought he saw the pouch drop to the tarmac, still gripped by the hand connected to what remained of his amputated forearm.

The second blade cut through his rib cage, carving a six-inch gash through his lungs.

The third blade continued through his upper torso, neatly cleaving him into two separate sections that seemed to remain joined where the incision touched.

The fourth blade lifted the top of Escobar's body away from his lower torso, leaving the lower trunk to crumble to the tarmac.

In the last flashing moments of life, riding above the whirlwind of the churning rotors, Escobar was turned toward the cockpit.

Through the flat armor glass of the rear tandem canopy, he saw a man staring coldly behind pursed lips.

Sacrette was throwing Escobar a kiss.

37

SACRETTE KNEW HE WAS IN THE HURT LOCKER THE
moment Escobar bolted for the ops building. Anger.
Frustration. Momentary brain failure. Or whatever the
hell else causes a well-disciplined man to step on his dick
seemed to happen all at once.

At least, he thought to himself, *the bastard was dead
and all he had to worry about was surviving the next eighteen
minutes, the amount of time he figured it would take to get out
of Cuban territory.*

But first things first.

"Get ready to recover the backpack!" Sacrette
shouted to Farnsworth as he banked forty-five degrees,
then hauled back on the collective, putting the Hind into
a tight turn.

Springing from the side door, Farnsworth grabbed
the pack, which was still clutched by the fingers of Escobar's severed arm. As he climbed back into the Hind,
the helo accelerated and banked sharply, slamming the
CPO against Dorffman, who lay on the floor, slobbering
in the fetal position.

"Get your guns ready, son!" Sacrette kicked at the
back of the weapons station below his seat.

Sisteros turned and looked up at the CAG. Sacrette nearly laughed. The young officer wore the most amazing look of confusion Sacrette had even seen.

"It's fuck, fight, or run a foot race, amigo. Maybe all three. So you get them goddamn weapons armed and ready." Sacrette raised a pistol and leveled the muzzle at the young Cuban's head. As the hammer came back, the trigger trembled.

Sisteros nodded weakly, then turned to the weapons console.

Skimming low over the tarmac, Sacrette changed course toward the main runway, then banked west.

Then he saw that the Cubans were starting to wake up to what was going on in their front yard.

"Take the helos at twelve o'clock. Give me a three-rocket spread. Then prepare for a 360 degree port turning assault." Sacrette pointed at a squadron of helicopters parked near the threshold of the main runway.

Neutralizing the cyclic, Sacrette hovered the Hind at twenty feet above the ground.

"Fire!" the CAG barked.

Sisteros pressed the firing switch. A 57mm rocket fired from the left rocket pod.

"Keep them coming, son. Pour it to them."

Two more rockets fired; then the Hind began a slow rotation to the left while hovering.

The air base began destructing in a growing circle of fire and explosions. Trucks were lifted in the air beneath the deadly rockets. The ops building disintegrated from a two-rocket spread. Four MiG-21 Fishbeds exploded, then disappeared in a black cloud of billowing, burning fuel.

In all, the attack lasted less than sixty seconds.

Amid chaos and confusion, Cuban troops fired, but the armor-plated Hind resisted the withering fire like a rhinoceros shaking off a pissant.

"Let's un-ass this locale, Thunderbolt," Farnsworth shouted from the starboard door where he manned a machine gun.

The CAG went to full power, then hauled back on the cyclic. Rising out of the black carpet of smoke that blanketed the airstrip, the Hind appeared like some prehistoric beast rising from a fuming volcano.

Slowly at first, then nose down, the "Devil's Chariot"—as it was called by Afghan freedom fighters—streaked thirty feet above the ground.

A long black vortex of smoke trailed the Hind to the edge of the runway, where Sacrette turned to a heading of 240 degrees as he dove the helo toward the deck.

Traveling nearly two hundred miles an hour at ten feet above the Caribbean, the Hind roared from the Gardens of the Queen toward the open water west of Cayo Caballones. Giant geysers of water exploded on the surface, leaving a rising signature in the Hind's wake.

Fourteen miles out, Sacrette popped up to three hundred feet; the Caribbean spread in every direction in green opalescence.

As he reached for the microphone, he noticed something gray and shining in the emerald-green sea.

38

THE FLIGHT DECK OF THE USS *VALIANT* NEVER looked more splendid. Eight F/A-18 Hornets waited in the parking area in front of the island, their wings folded, waiting to roll onto one of the four catapults when ordered.

At Alert Five, four Hornets were cocked in the shuttle; the clamshell canopies were open, the pilots buckled in and ready to launch.

"Battle stations. All hands report to battle stations," the voice of the air boss boomed over the 1-MC intercom on the flight deck.

Gun crews wearing flak jackets and helmets raced from the island, charging head down across the flight deck. Reaching the catwalk encircling the deck of the carrier, the men disappeared from view into the many .50-calibre machine gun and radar-guided 20mm cannon turrets ringing the carrier.

In his cockpit at Alert Five, Domino closed the canopy, saluted, then waited for the pressure to build in the bow catapult.

Forward of the Hornet, a glassed-in bubble rose eighteen inches above the deck between the two Strike/

Fighters. Sitting in the catapult control bubble, the cat officer watched the pressure gauges rise. When sufficient power had been reached, he pressed a button, releasing the steam-powered piston.

The roar of Domino's engines ricocheted off the blast deflector shield, sending a hot, scorching burst of exhaust into the air. On the buzzard's perch, the heat rose in rippling waves.

Less than three seconds after the cat officer launched Wolf Two, Domino was one hundred yards beyond the bow of the *Valiant*, raising his nose while banking left.

From the CIC, the Air Ops officer vectored Domino to his heading. "Wolf Two . . . turn to zero-nine-zero. We have an inbound bogey at fourteen miles. Intercept and identify."

Domino rolled onto the heading; Caveman had the radar humming in the pit.

"Got him, Domino," Caveman called as the blip appeared on his screen.

"Lock him up, Caveman. I'll try to make a visual."

"Not much time, Domino. He's approaching the carrier low and mean-looking."

Domino spotted the Hind's geysering signature off the water before he saw the camouflage-painted gunship.

"Jesus!" Domino exclaimed. "It's a Hind!"

"What's a Russian helo doing coming this close to the battle group?" Caveman asked.

"No time to find out. Let's rock 'n' roll!" Domino replied.

Switching the weapons system to cannon, Domino peeled off to the starboard, then swung back onto the Hind's nine o'clock port wing position.

As he pressed the firing switch, a long tongue of 20mm cannon fire joined the Hornet to the surface, just ahead of the Hind's nose section.

"You better chill out, buddy," Domino called to the threatening helo.

As though it could hear him, the Hind slowed to a hover.

"Put them on camera," Domino ordered.

As the F/A-18 shot past on another warning run, the television cameras flashed the Hind onto the middle display.

"I'll be a son of a bitch!" Caveman shouted joyfully.

The radio crackled from the CIC; in the background, the men monitoring Wolf Three's television transmission were shouting excitedly.

"Hold your fire, Wolf Three." The voice of Admiral Lord stopped Domino's finger from applying the last bit of needed pressure.

Domino began a slow rotation around the Hind at minimum controllable airspeed.

Domino spoke to Admiral Lord, "You're got to give the men a shot of this, Admiral."

"They're getting it now . . . live, and in color."

Lord glanced at the television set in the CIC. Throughout the *Valiant*, all eyes were glued to the opened port-side door of the Russian gunship.

CPO Diamonds Farnsworth knelt in the opened door.

Wearing a broad grin, he was taking a leak.

PART THREE: GULF RAIDERS

39

1430.

THE LUXURY YACHT *CRISTOBAL* TUGGED LIGHTLY AT a mooring buoy in the bay; overhead, the shriek of sea gulls pierced the air, echoing over the aqua-blue swimming pool on the fantail.

Joaquin Zarante sat in a leather chaise lounge; sweat dripped from his shoulders to his stomach, to his loins, where a young blond woman licked the perspiration with red, full lips.

He felt like an Incan king, except now his power was greater than his ancestors'. His was the greatest power: the power of fear. He would have the weapon to stand off his enemies.

He would have the courage to use the weapon, unlike others he once thought had power.

Raising a glass, he drank, then stroked the blond mane, which brought him momentary pleasure. When he felt the orgasm, he laughed until the wave of ecstasy receded, then took the woman by the hair.

She was young, beautiful. Touching a button on the telephone beside his chair, he turned and watched the sea. In the distance, a ship floated on the surface.

He had watched the ship for days, but didn't fear its presence.

What was there to fear? he asked himself. *It was merely a ship. He was a king.*

An Incan king ready to strike the Americans who would try to destroy him, and his family of the Sendero Luminoso. No one could destroy him, except SPANISH—the "Council of the Old Ones."

He had been warned; they counseled against what he was doing. They didn't want their power to extend beyond the Huallaga. The Huallaga was sufficient. They only wanted to grow cocaine. As their ancestors had for centuries.

Zarante wanted more. And he knew that more meant greater risk.

As he looked up, a bodyguard appeared. He was short, broad-shouldered, and evil-looking, the mark of manhood in the Huallaga.

Pulling the girl up by the hair, he said to the bodyguard, "Take her to the crew. My gift for the afternoon."

The bodyguard took her arm. Her vacant eyes twitched, then settled. She didn't appear to know where she was. Or what was happening.

Zarante dialed a number from memory, then waited. A secretary answered, and hearing his name pressed another button in her Havana office, connecting Zarante with a voice he recognized.

"My informants have delivered disturbing news, Generalissimo." Zarante pouted another glass of cognac as he spoke. "News of Colonel Escobar's death. Is this true? Is he dead?"

There was a pause from Havana. Confirmation followed.

"I need assurance, Generalissimo," said Zarante.

"What kind of assurance?" the voice asked.

"Assurance that our project has not been compromised."

"You have my assurance." The voice from Havana sounded confident. "The incident involved two pilots who were shot down during an American attack on our air force. Colonel Escobar was taking part in the search for the Americans."

Zarante sipped the cognac. His black eyes flashed, then he asked the question that wouldn't be easily explained. "What about Dorffman?"

Another pause; this pause was longer, strained. "Dorffman is missing."

Zarante sat forward. His face twisted with anger. He wanted to scream, but he forced himself to remember that he was talking to a powerful man. A man he needed, if only for the next few hours. "Your fools have placed our project in jeopardy."

"Nothing is jeopardized. What can their government do? It's their word against mine. The Americans have a scientist from East Germany. A scientist they can't prove was in Cuba. Like all the times before . . . they will sit on their hands."

Knowing the American government and how often the generalissimo had made them look foolish in the past brought Zarante some reassurance. "Perhaps you're right."

"Our relationship is still protected," the generalissimo added. "Dorffman's assistants are now in charge. Your product will be delivered as agreed."

Zarante recalled the metal box Dorffman took from the safe. He could clearly see the two empty holes. He recalled Dorffman's explanation.

Why was Escobar looking for two American pilots?

Why was Dorffman with him?

There was no logical answer; however, if the Americans did know about the plant, he would have to move fast. A new plant could be built. In another country. Money was no problem. Not now. Not yet.

"Instruct your personnel at Campo Viramo I will arrive there tonight to take delivery of the first installment."

"How will you travel?"

"By seaplane." With that, Zarante hung up the telephone.

He drained the cognac, then pressed a button on the telephone console. A gruff voice answered.

"Send me the redhead. The one with the tattoo on her thigh." Releasing the button, he bent to the table. A solid gold saucer brimmed with a white, powdery substance. Taking a small spoon, he dipped into the tray. A quick snort followed.

Pouring another glass of cognac, he shivered when the warm glow from the coca threaded through his senses. As the redhead appeared from the salon belowdeck, he turned and raised his glass to the ship sitting on the horizon.

On the horizon a superstructure could be seen rising above the upper deck of the ship.

The USS *Valiant*.

40

1500.

"WELCOME BACK, CAPTAIN SACRETTE." ADMIRAL Lord walked briskly into the sick bay followed by a marine. The weathery face of the admiral was spread in a broad smile.

From his seat on the examination table, Sacrette laughed lightly at hearing his new rank from the admiral. "That new title will take some getting used to . . . Admiral."

Sacrette extended his hand to Lord. "Congratulations, Admiral Lord."

Lord turned to Farnsworth. "Chief Farnsworth." They shook hands. "Well done."

"Congratulations, Admiral. Thank you. It's good to be back on friendly ground."

Lord turned to a smaller figure sitting beside Sacrette on the examination table. "And who might this be?"

Cucho was staring wide-eyed at the admiral, as he had stared in awe at everything he had seen since arriving aboard the carrier. He was holding a can of Coca-Cola. Offering the soda pop to Lord, he replied, "My name is Cucho."

Lord politely shook his head to the soda pop; to Sacrette, he raised his eyebrows questioningly. "Is this boy Cuban?"

Sacrette shrugged. "Not anymore. He can't go back to Cuba. Not after what he's done for us. And what he's seen."

Lord smiled reassuringly at the boy. Then to Sacrette he said, "Fill me in on your activities since you went down."

Fifteen minutes later Sacrette had completed his report to Admiral Lord.

"Where is Dorffman?" Lord asked.

"Two SPs are watching over him in the brig." Sacrette laughed. "He's asking for diplomatic immunity."

Lord wasn't surprised. "That's out of our hands. But first, where is the chemical evidence?"

Sacrette reached beneath the table; taking the metallic sphere from the backpack, he showed it to Cucho. "Okay if I give this to the admiral?"

Cucho nodded.

Lord looked warily at the sphere. "I'll get this to our intelligence officer. It'll be on its way to Washington in fifteen minutes."

"A Peruvian drug cartel is behind the operation, Admiral. They've got something planned. What it is, I don't know. But they've sunk a lot of money into the Cuban government." Sacrette spoke while stretching; the bruises on his bare chest were blue from the ordeal.

"We'll let intel take it upstairs. Meanwhile, we've got our hands full." Lord glanced at Farnsworth.

"My aircraft?" Sacrette asked.

"Affirmative." Turning to the marine corporal standing at the door, Lord nodded his head. "I have a surprise for you, Chief."

Before Farnsworth could ask, a familiar voice called from the door.

"Hello, Pop." Lt. Daniel Farnsworth walked hurriedly toward his father.

"I'll be damned," Farnsworth whispered, reaching for his son.

They embraced; Daniel shook hands with Sacrette.

"Tell me about the recovery operation," Sacrette said to Lord.

For the next ten minutes, Lord briefed both Sacrette and the CPO on Operation Bold Forager.

"Bold Forager is a good name, alright," said Sacrette. "Bold is what we'll have to be. That area is stirred up like a hornet's nest. Pardon the pun."

Lord appeared confident. "The battle group is swinging on line. The E-2 Hawkeye will fly AWAC; the EF-111A will fly electronic countermeasures, giving the air wing a jamming platform if needed. We'll use the Viking squadron to jam up Cuban coastal radar and mines in the gulf."

Sacrette looked at Daniel. "Are your boys ready?"

Daniel grinned. "Semper Fi. We're always ready."

Diamonds beamed at his son. Looking at Sacrette, he said, "Not bad for a jarhead, huh, Captain?"

Sacrette laughed. "Not bad. Not bad at all."

Not bad, Sacrette said to himself. *Terrific! What a pair*.

Lord pointed a finger at the CAG. "Captain Sacrette. Get cleaned up. Catch some chow. We'll have a final briefing at twenty-hundred. The balloon goes up at twenty-two-hundred." As he turned, Lord took Cucho's hand. "Thank you, Cucho."

As Lord walked away, Sacrette asked, "What about

the plant? We should launch an air strike, sir."

Lord looked troubled by the thought. "Running a covert operation inside Cuba is one thing, Captain. Launching an air strike is another. We'll wait for a decision from the president. But, be ready."

"Yes, sir," Sacrette replied. Turning to Diamonds, he told the CPO, "Let's get off our butts and back in the game. We've got a mission."

Farnsworth cast his head lightly toward Cucho. "What about the boy?"

"We'll have to wait and see," Sacrette said as he walked out of the sick bay. Daniel and Diamonds couldn't help but note the sadness in Sacrette's voice, and in his eyes.

In his quarters four decks below the sick bay, Sacrette dropped onto his bunk. Fatigue had drained him to nothing but raw nerves. As he tried to take a nap, a gnawing edginess pulled at him.

Sitting upright, he shook his head, then said aloud, "Nerves, hell. It's not nerves."

He knew what was troubling him. There was only one thing he could think of at the moment.

Taking the telephone, he dialed the communications center on the *Valiant*, gave the technician a telephone number, then leaned back while the microwave connection was joined by satellite.

Thirty seconds later a man with a low voice answered.

Sacrette took a deep breath and, knowing he didn't need to identify himself, said to the voice, "I've got a problem. I need your help."

41

1600.

ON AN AIRCRAFT CARRIER THE MOST CRITICAL SHORT-age—other than women—is space; especially parking space for the nearly one hundred aircraft composing the air wing. Other than the flight deck, where most aircraft are parked, the hangar deck serves as a supplemental parking area, maintenance area, and general hang-out area for both pilots and crew.

The most instantly recognizable aspect of the hangar deck is the constant noise, along with the smell and taste of aviation oil. All of which assault the senses brutally.

For newly promoted—and returned—Captain Boulton Sacrette, the underworld of the hangar deck rang with a din, and reeked with a miasma that he found glorious and refreshing.

Prancing along the metal-floor deck, he was the picture of a sharp military commander. He was freshly shaved, his close-cropped hair brushed back; his boots were shined to a high spit-shine polish. Wearing a pressed flight suit, he seemed to delight in the sound of the snapping and popping where the fabric rubbed at his thighs.

Stopping at each of the various squadron areas, Sacrette spent several minutes with the skippers, then moved along the line of parked airplanes, pausing occasionally to admire their beauty and individuality.

He noted the SH-60B Seahawk anti-submarine warfare helicopters, with their magnet anomaly detectors attached to the MAD housing on the starboard fuselage's fixed pylon.

And gazed admiringly at the Navy's miniaturized version of the AWAC, the Grumman E-2 Hawkeyes, their wings folded beneath the distinctive discus-shaped rotodome, where APS-125 ARPS provided the battle group its first line of defense against air attack through the eyes of the E-2's advanced radar processing system.

Eight F-14 Tomcats, the air wing's long-range fighter punch, which Sacrette had flown before choosing the F/A-18 Hornet Strike/Fighter.

Six Grumman KA-6D Intruders, the former strike aircraft now converted to service the F/A-18 Strike/Fighters as a rocket-packing refueling tanker.

Ten Lockheed S-3 Vikings, hot ASW mini-jets that could sense and attack submarines thousands of miles from the core of the battle group.

But, as always, it was when reaching the aft section of the hangar deck that Sacrette changed his pace and strolled slowly in and out of the "tits machines" parked in a tight group.

The Strike/Fighters of VFA-101.

Resting with their wings folded at their joints, the fighters looked like inverted pterodactyls waiting to rise and challenge the sky.

Sleek. Awesome. Deadly. Supersonic swift.

Painted in low-visibility gray, each fighter carried the emblem of a fighting hornet on the tail, which resembled the fighting Irishman of Notre Dame football.

"Thunderbolt!" A shout seemed to rise above the din, silencing the noise for a moment as all eyes turned to the CAG.

His running name echoed through the deck, and he couldn't help but feel the goose bumps rise on his arms. Coming toward him were dozens of the young sailors who kept the fighting machines in the air. The maintenance crew. The bomb loaders. Plane captains. Cat crew. Signal operators.

The soul of the aircraft carrier's air wing.

"The CAG is back!" one young sailor shouted; he walked toward Sacrette, wiping his fingers with an oily rag. Stopping three feet away, the young man snapped to attention and saluted.

Sacrette returned the salute and, as always, flashed the grin every airdale on the carrier would recognize in a hurricane.

"It's about time you came back to work!" Chief Petty Officer Diamonds Farnsworth boomed from behind the crowding maintenance crew.

As the gathering parted, Diamonds stepped through the opening. Walking beside him was Lt. Commander Harris "Weasel" Jones, the air wing maintenance officer, and the only man Sacrette trusted to oversee the Hornet contingency.

"I told you not to trust those damn jarheads at China Lake," Jones chided, extending his hand to the CAG.

Sacrette winced, remembering that the China Lake marine mechanics had maintained the Hornet now resting in the Blue Hole of Reina.

Shaking hands, he nearly blushed at the short, skinny MO. "You can bet it's the last time, Weasel."

Diamonds reached into the crowd and pulled at a

small hand. "Look who's come in for an inspection."

"Thunderbolt," said the excited Cucho. "Diamonds is showing me your dugout."

Sacrette's mind flashed back to the cave beneath the tree on French Soldier's Point. As he looked around, he realized that the hangar deck was a sort of dugout like Cucho's. A place to come home to.

Sacrette looked at Daniel. "I understand your team is going to recover my aircraft."

Daniel glanced at his watch. "We jump off at twenty-two-hundred. Your boys will be standing by to give us TAC CAP if the area heats up."

Sacrette shook his head dejectedly. "Not me. Unless I can sprout wings and carry a missile in my teeth."

"Sir. We were just about to head for the chow hall. This boy hasn't had a decent meal in days. Not to mention yours truly," said Farnsworth. "But first . . . I want you to see something."

Walking though the crowd, Farnsworth approached one of the F/A-18B single-seat Hornets. The radome hung open at the hinge; the canopy jutted open at an angle.

Farnsworth climbed the ladder of the single-seat fighter. His hand disappeared into the cockpit, then reappeared, holding a helmet mounted with a device Sacrette recognized.

"The hoot owl eyes and other equipment came in while we were vacationing in Cuba," said the CPO.

"Where did this aircraft come from?" asked Sacrette.

"The captain . . . I mean, the admiral had it ferried over from the RAG at Jacksonville the morning after we went down. She's all ready to fly," Farnsworth said.

Weasel leaned to Sacrette and whispered, "The men did the paint job."

Farnsworth swept the helmet equipped with the "Cat's Eyes" night goggles toward the twin rudder tail section.

A wave of soft laughter drifted through the men as they saw Sacrette's eyes narrow on the toed-in port tail rudder, where the number was painted in black.

Zero. Zero.

The double nuts of the CAG.

42

1645.

SERVING OVER EIGHTEEN THOUSAND MEALS A DAY, the mess service of the *Valiant* was one of the busiest services on board the carrier. If the sailors had a single expectation that was never violated, it was knowing the food would be delicious. To offer anything less would lower morale, and possibly invite mutiny from the men who were often at sea for months at a time.

Two main dining halls, or "messes," located fore and aft served the enlisted crew, except for the CPOs, who had their own mess. Officers ate in three different dining areas called ward rooms. Aboard the *Valiant*, the battle group commander enjoyed the luxury of his own admiral's mess, but the men know Admiral Lord would generally be found eating in the ward rooms, or in his sea cabin.

Detractors of the military often criticized this time-honored tradition as being discriminatory, as establishing a caste system, and, therefore, costing the taxpayers a great deal of extra dollars that could be saved by having one dining area for all ranks.

Perhaps it would work, thought newly promoted Captain Boulton Sacrette, who was sitting in the enlisted

forward mess. But it wasn't the need to discuss dining
protocol that brought him here, nor the hundreds of other
officers and enlisted men in the standing-room-only gathering.

At that moment, in the dining hall adjacent to the
galley, where the food was cooked, the prestige of the
Valiant's mess was now being tested by a new arrival.

Near the center of the dining hall, Lt. Marvin
"Caveman" Zak floated into the seat beside Domino, grinning at the VFA-101 exec. Leaning sideways, the exec's
RIO whispered, "We've got a pool taking bets on how
long the kid lasts."

Domino was watching the scrawny figure at the end
of the table. Turning to Caveman, he placed his bet.
"Put me down for twenty. I say the kid makes it all the
way through the apple pie."

Sitting next to Domino, Sacrette shook his head.
"I've got fifty that says he goes the distance and eats
two pieces of apple pie."

"Holy moley," Caveman breathed in astonishment.
"Look at that boy eat."

Cucho Clemente, who sat between CPO Diamonds
Farnsworth and Lt. Daniel Farnsworth at the end of a
long table draped in a white cloth, was the focal point
of attention.

Surrounded by food, Cucho attacked a turkey drum-
stick he held in one hand; while holding a fork in the
other, he speared bits of boiled carrots, mashed potatoes,
candied yams, and creamed corn.

To the delight of the mess officer, a short, rotund
lieutenant commander whose running name was tradi-
tionally "Spoon," the boy was literally an eating machine. And a delight to behold.

Domino chuckled. "Quite a kid you've got there, Thunderbolt. He appears to have a fondness for Spoon's groceries."

Sacrette beamed like the father of a newborn. "We wouldn't have made it out of Cuba without him. Hell. He shot a Cuban soldier... saved Farnsworth's life."

Domino shook his head, recalling their escape from Castroland. "You and Diamonds must live right."

Nodding at Cucho, Sacrette said, "Living right had nothing to do with it. We were lucky. Damn lucky."

"Yeah. A lot luckier than Blade and Axeman."

Sacrette shifted his attention away from Cucho to the exec. "I'm not going to give you one of those horse-shit lectures about how 'You've got to get over this,' or 'You did your best.' That's a lot of crap. It happened. They're dead. I buried them. Me, the chief, and the kid. That's the bottom line."

Domino couldn't smile away the sadness reflected in his eyes. He squeezed Sacrette's wrist appreciatively. "I know. But that doesn't make it any easier."

Sacrette sat back and ran a hand over his face roughly; fatigue had pulled the soft tissue beneath his eyes into drooping bags. He wanted to forget about the dead pilots. He wanted to rejoice at being alive. He wanted to watch Diamonds and Daniel watch Cucho eat the tablecloth off the table.

Instead, he knew there was something he needed to say to the exec. "It's not supposed to be easy. If it were easy to watch your men die, you wouldn't be here. If it sounds hard-assed, it's because it has to be hard-assed. We're throwing these kids up against the toughest technology in the world. And they're supposed to all come out alive? No way. We've been lucky. Be glad for the ones who survived because you were there. Keeping them alive will give you more than enough to think about."

Before Domino could respond, the 1-MC intercom boomed.

"Captain Sacrette. Report to the admiral's sea cabin."

Sacrette walked around to where Cucho was sitting. The boy's cheeks bulged as though he were a squirrel with a mouthful of hickory nuts.

"Chief, you can stow this character in my cabin for the night. But first, Doc Holweigner wants to give him a physical. Take him to sick bay."

Cucho stopped chewing; his eyes seemed to shine as he realized something he had feared since arriving aboard the carrier.

"Will I see you again, Thunderbolt? I know I can't stay on your boat."

Sacrette's mouth tightened. "Ship. It's a ship. You put boats on a ship. You can't put a ship on a boat."

The boy looked confused.

Sacrette's mouth relaxed in a smile. "You'll see me again. More than you think. If it's what you want."

"What do you mean, Thunderbolt?" Cucho asked.

"I called someone I know in America. Someone I trust. He wants you to come live with him. I'm sure the State Department can make the arrangements."

"In Oakland?"

Sacrette shook his head. "No. Montana."

43

"I WANT YOU TO HEAR SOMETHING." ADMIRAL LORD ushered Sacrette into his sea cabin while glaring at Dorffman, who stood surrounded by three large marines.

Standing behind the marines were two men. Sacrette didn't recognize their faces, but he knew instinctively what they were.

Pointing at a short, stocky-built man in bush khakis with close-cropped hair, Lord introduced, "Colonel Samuel Travers. Colonel Travers is with the US Embassy in Kingston. He's the operations officer for a special drug task force in the Caribbean."

Travers introduced the man standing beside him. "This is Mr. Conyers. Conyers is with the DEA."

Conyers was dressed casually; he had long, neatly trimmed hair and a Vandyke beard. His fingers sparkled beneath diamond rings; on his wrist, an expensive Phillip Patek watch was barely visible beneath the cuff of his silk shirt. To Sacrette, he appeared to fit the image of the kind of people the DEA would be chasing.

"What's up?" Sacrette asked Lord.

Conyers answered the question. "In short . . . Joaquin Zarante."

"The man who runs the Sindero?" Sacrette remembered the name given by Escobar.

Conyers nodded, then continued, "Zarante is the field leader of the Sindero. Their action man. In actuality, the Sindero is overseen by a group of elders called 'the Council of the Old Ones.' The Council never comes out of those Peruvian jungles. Zarante is the man who does all the legwork."

"You want Zarante," Sacrette said flatly.

"That's correct," said Travers. "It's the first opportunity we've had to nail the bastard outside Peru, which means it's the first opportunity. Period. He's untouchable once he gets back to the Huallaga Valley."

Sacrette looked at Dorffman. "Do you know where he is?"

Dorffman shook his head weakly. It was apparent to Sacrette that the German was in deeper than he had bargained for. "No. I only know he intends to come to the facility tonight. To pick up the first shipment of the chemicals."

Sacrette looked at his watch. "What time?"

Dorffman shrugged. "Midnight. He always comes at midnight."

"How?" asked Sacrette.

"Usually by airplane. A seaplane. He is picked up near the beach by a boat, then is brought by jeep to the camp."

Sacrette began to understand. Looking at Travers, he asked, "What do you have in mind?"

"We don't know where he is at this moment. He could be anywhere. But if we know where he's going to be, we can be waiting."

"Cuba? Tonight?" Sacrette saw the conflict. "We

have a mission scheduled for tonight. Trying to grab Zarante could cost us the whole operation. Why not just wait until midnight, then flatten Campo Viramo with an air strike? We can kill two birds with one hellacious stone."

Lord answered the question. "The president has expressed his reluctance to give us the go-ahead on an air strike."

"Reluctance?" Sacrette snapped. "The president seems reluctant to do anything. His reluctance cost us Noriega when we had the opportunity in October. Reluctance! Hell. The president declares war on drugs, then throws in the towel at the first opportunity to win a major battle. That's not reluctance. That's bullshit!"

There was a momentary silence.

"That's enough of your insubordination, Captain Sacrette." Lord's voice was firm, but Sacrette could see the reflection of agreement in the admiral's eyes.

Travers turned to Sacrette. "We now have another opportunity within our grasp. If we can get Zarante . . . that would be a score nearly as big as Noriega."

Sacrette could see there would be no argument. "What about the Hornet?"

Admiral Lord went to a map on his desk. He tapped the area lying within the Gulf of Guacanayabo. "Bold Forager goes ahead as scheduled. We'll run a parallel operation against Zarante. The timing and the location are proximal. Zarante will be in the area."

Sacrette examined the map. Finally, he asked, "How do you plan to take down Zarante?"

For the next ten minutes, Sacrette listened to the plan. When Conyers finished laying out the operation against Zarante, the CAG turned to Admiral Lord. "It could work. But what if he slips through?"

Lord smiled devilishly. "In that event, Mr. Zarante will be your responsibility."

Putting on his blue hat emblazoned with gold aviator wings and the words TOP GUN, Sacrette nodded coldly. As he started for the door, he said, "My pleasure."

In the VFA-101 maintenance area, Sacrette found Chief Farnsworth overseeing the preparation of the fighters.

"Rigged and ready, Captain," said Farnsworth.

"Fighter mode?" Sacrette asked.

Farnsworth nodded. He noticed the CAG was acting nervous; perhaps it was the mission.

"I want one minor change." Pointing at a weapons carrier, Sacrette told the CPO, "I want this baby put on my aircraft."

Farnsworth stared at the weapon. A variety of thoughts began running through his head. All led to one conclusion: disaster.

"I can't let you take that weapon, sir. It's not authorized on the ordnance manifest." Farnsworth knew what the CAG would say before the words were out of his mouth.

"Put it on the aircraft, Chief. I'll take care of the manifest." Sacrette was staring coldly at Farnsworth.

Farnsworth nodded reluctantly. "Aye, aye, Skipper."

As Sacrette started to walk away, Farnsworth asked, "What about Castro? He'll pitch a shitfit if you're planning what I think you're planning."

Sacrette's face hardened as he turned and looked at the weapon. "To hell with Castro!"

Farnsworth shouted to Sacrette. "What about your career?"

"To hell with my career," the CAG retorted as he disappeared through the door leading to the island.

Farnsworth shook his head angrily.

Ten minutes later Sacrette's aircraft was ready for combat. Wiping the oil from his hands, Farnsworth studied the sleek fighter.

"What the hell. It don't mean nothing."

He, too, had made a decision.

Dropping the oily rag, he went in search of the one person he knew could get him into the action.

44

2158.

"ADMIRAL'S ON THE BRIDGE!" A STONE-FACED MARINE corporal barked as Admiral Lord entered the bridge.

Seating himself in his starboard chair, Lord smoothed the fatigue from his face, then checked his watch. Outside the bridge, the electrical whine of the four massive elevators bringing aircraft to the flight deck seemed to buzz constantly.

The hair on Lord's neck prickled from the roaring thunder as the E-2 Hawkeye bolted from Cat One, signaling the commencement of Operation Bold Forager. Within seconds the "eyes of the battle group" was outbound to its station off Grand Cayman, where the discus-shaped radar mounted atop the fuselage would track air activity over the entire Caribbean.

"Launch the F-18s," the voice of the admiral called over the 1-MC flight deck intercom.

Streaks of fire shot into the sky; sleek, needle-nosed fighters rode on a carpet of flame as twelve aircraft catapulted toward their station off Puerto Rico.

All but one.

Unlike the F-14 Tomcats, or F-4 Phantoms, the

F-18s didn't require Zone Five afterburner thrust for launch; carrying a light load void of bombs, the Hornets could launch from standard military power.

Gripping the HOTAS, Sacrette didn't go to Zone Five, but he did increase power slightly to offset the added weight he was carrying under his right wing.

When the cat officer fired the launch shuttle, Sacrette felt his body slam into the seat. Seconds later he was easing back on the HOTAS, then banked right, raised the nose, and shot straight up toward the stars.

"Wolf One . . . departing for station Baker. Wolf Pack . . . fly to Alpha station and stand by."

Reaching Angels eighteen, Sacrette turned north. Through his "Cat's Eyes," the night and sea were blue-green. In the distance, off the right wing, he could see Cuba.

Switching to the crypto frequency, he contacted what would be the first of the Americans to penetrate Cuban territory.

"*Gulf Raider* . . . this is Wolf One. Proceed to station Tango."

The voice of Cody McKuen replied softly in the CAG's ear, "Roger, Wolf One. *Gulf Raider* outbound from Zulu station to station Tango. See you if we need you."

Looking back quickly. Sacrette saw the tiny craft through his night-vision goggles; the *Raider* was turning east, skimming over the surface like an eagle.

What he didn't see was the fiery signature south of the battle group; a burning exhaust from another craft moving out of Montego Bay.

45

JOAQUIN ZARANTE'S BLACK EYES BURNED FROM BE-
hind the Plexiglas bubble of the helmet covering his
head. He was sitting in a cockpit, adjusting power throttles while watching a moving map display on the console.

Carefully he fine-tuned the display until he had the
Jardines de la Reina framed on the screen. After com-
puterizing his course, he tuned a radio frequency known
only to him and the Cuban patrol vessel that would be
waiting near French Soldier's Point.

He keyed the mike once, then twice in rapid suc-
cession.

The signal had been given.

Seconds later the squelch broke three times over his
headphones. The Cuban response signaling he had been
received.

Zarante leaned back, lightly gripping the stick.
Glancing to the right seat, his lips curled cruelly as he
gazed at a heavy metal object propped against the con-
toured bucket of the plush leather seat.

He reached and patted the Stinger rocket; the metal
felt cool against his skin.

The power felt exhilarating.

Reminding him of what power he would have in less than twenty-four hours.

"Your plan is very dangerous," he had been warned earlier by one of the Council.

"Danger is a necessary part of our business," he had replied sharply. "The Americans will destroy us, as they are destroying the Colombians. We must have a weapon. Fear is our only weapon. They will know the meaning of fear in twenty-four hours."

The old man on the Council cautioned him, "It is one thing to kill an enemy. It is another thing to attack a great nation in such a manner as you have planned."

Zarante refused to listen. "The plan is already in motion. The message will be delivered tomorrow. I will have the bacteria in Miami by eight o'clock in the morning. An airplane is waiting to take me to San Francisco. Nothing can go wrong."

"Yes," agreed the old man. "But perhaps you go too far. Many people will die!"

"Yes," he said aloud. Many people will die. Then the Americans will pull back. The Huallaga will not be a target. Nor the Sindero.

He shoved the throttles forward; a blast from the engines thundered the craft along.

Flying only inches above the water, Zarante laughed, then said aloud, "It will be a memorable World Series. A World Series of death!"

46

Aboard the *Gulf Raider*, Lt. Commander Quinton Turk stood at the controls, constantly checking gauges, listening to the purr of the engines, which were pushing the hydrofoil well past one hundred knots.

Standing behind Turk, Lt. Daniel Farnsworth was dressed in a black neoprene wetsuit; beside Daniel stood Travers and Conyers, both dressed in camouflage fatigues.

"I'd better go aft and check on my men, sir," Daniel told Turk.

Walking out onto the weather deck, Daniel was pummeled by a hundred-knot windblast. A lifeline ran fore and aft, the only means of keeping from being blown off the deck. Holding on to the lifeline, Daniel slowly allowed himself to be slid along the deck as the wind pushed him along from behind.

On the rear deck, a blast shield vented the prop blast upward, allowing the Kiowa to sit in a relatively wind-free environment, held steady by the RAST, the recover-assist-secure-traverse system that enabled the helo to be winched into its securing station from a hovering attitude.

The UDT men were sitting by their equipment

beneath the Kiowa. As he approached his men, Daniel suddenly stopped in his tracks.

"What in the hell are you doing here!" Daniel demanded.

Stepping from behind the helo, Chief Petty Officer Diamonds Farnsworth approached his son wearing a grin.

And a wetsuit.

"Lending my years of expertise to this mission," Diamonds replied.

Daniel's eyes burned with anger. "You are AWOL, Chief Farnsworth."

"I'm here, Lieutenant Farnsworth," Diamonds shouted over the howl of the windblast. "You're going to need all the help you can get. You're running a double-edged operation inside enemy territory. Besides, I know precisely where the bird is located in the blue hole. I rode her down. Remember? And furthermore, someone's going to have to operate the controls during ascent. That'll be my job. I know that aircraft better than any man alive."

Daniel's eyes began searching the rear deck; through the watery mist enveloping the area, he found the man he knew was responsible for his father being aboard the *Raider*. "Chief Lovgren, I'm going to throw your muscle-bound ass in the brig when we get back. If we get back!"

Saying nothing more, Daniel turned and began pulling himself along the lifeline leading through the teeth of a hundred-mile-an-hour blast of wet air.

As Daniel stormed off, CPO Lovgren walked meekly to Diamonds's side; he was wearing a short-sleeved wetsuit top over bulging biceps that twitched nervously. His body was soaked, as were the other men sitting in the constant spray.

"Christ, Diamonds," Lovgren shouted. "I told you he would burn my ass!"

Diamonds smiled. Leaning to Lovgren's ear, he shouted, "Remember that VC whore that tried to kill you in Danang?"

Lovgren nodded. Through the slick film on his face, a smile appeared. "Yeah. I owe you one."

Diamonds extended his wet hand to Lovgren. "Consider the books as being square."

As he took Farnsworth's hand, the UDT man watched Daniel disappear onto the weather deck. "He's really got a case of the ass."

"He'll get over it," replied Diamonds, running his hands over his slick pate.

"I don't know."

"I do. I know that boy better than you. I used to change his messy diapers."

47

2245.

LT. WILLIS COLE'S FACE WAS PAINTED AN EERIE OR-
ange from the magenta glow of the suppressed lighting
illuminating the *Gulf Raider*'s bridge. As he started to sip
from his coffee cup, his hands stopped inches from his
mouth as the lines of an island came into view on his
forward-looking infrared digital moving map display.

"Skipper. We've got the Reina islands off the port
bow. Twenty nautical miles at zero-three-zero."

"Roger," replied Skip Turk. "Execute three-
hundred-sixty-degree holding pattern. I'll touch base
with the Sea Dragon."

In the cockpit of his MH-53E Sea Dragon, Lt. Jack
Kilpatrick heard the request from Lt. Commander Turk.

"*Gulf Raider* requesting a slot."

"Roger, *Gulf Raider*," Kilpatrick responded. "Stand
by."

Flying at minimum controllable airspeed, Kilpatrick's massive minesweeping helo churned the black sea
beneath his fuselage into a whipping caldron. Four
hundred feet behind, held by heavy cable, an MK 166
magnetic information sledge supported on hydrofoil

blades followed in tight tow.

The sledge, an electronic wonder, could detect and clear mines by magnetic anomaly, accoustic sensory, pressure contact, or mechanical impact.

Kilpatrick didn't want to detonate the mine field he knew was guarding the Cuban coast. Rather, he merely wanted to target the mines for the *Raider* as it approached the Blue Hole of Reina.

As he activated the FLIR on the heads-up display, then punched in his computer the screen he would use to observe the mines targeted by the sledge was instantly transmitted in real time to the computer display in the *Raider*.

Switching to "whisper," Kilpatrick muffled the enormous noise emitted by his nearly four-thousand-horse-power twin engines.

Pushing the nose down from a higher angle of attack, he felt the acceleration in ground effect as the airspeed zoomed from less than one hundred to the red-line max at nearly two hundred miles an hour.

From the sledge, the mine-detecting sensors swept the Gulf of Guacanayabo.

At his console in the *Raider*, Cole saw the electronic mines begin to light up on the display as the Sea Dragon plotted a path through the deadly mine field.

"Zero-eight-five," Cole's calm voice reported.

Quinton Turk turned to port on the heading, then waited for the next correction.

Another signature etched the display screen.

"One-one-five." Cole's nose was nearly touching the screen as the *Raider* ran an avoidance pattern through the killer gauntlet.

The *Raider* swung to starboard.

"Zero-seven-zero."

The *Raider* swung to port at over one hundred knots.

The signals came rapidly; the course changes were sudden, dramatic, nearly throwing the UDT from the rear deck as the pugnacious *Raider* charged lightning swift through the Cuban defenses.

Undetected.

Glancing at the digital display five minutes into the penetration, Cole looked up.

Quinton Turk recognized the expression on Cole's face. He didn't need to hear the words.

Months of training had drilled that instinctive recognition into each person aboard the *Gulf Raider*; you could read the thoughts of the crew members in a flash in their glowing red eyes.

The *Gulf Raider* was sitting above the Blue Hole of Reina.

Taking the microphone, Turk called to the rear deck where Lt. Daniel Farnsworth, his UDT team, and CPO Diamonds Farnsworth sat waiting for the command to launch them into the Blue Hole of Reina.

"Insert! Insert! Insert!"

In the next instance, Turk pulled back on the throttles; the bow of the *Raider* rose, then nosed forward into a surging wall of water as the craft settled against its own energy.

On the rear deck, the UDT personnel felt the surge. Equipment went over the side; then the men followed.

As he hit the water, CPO Diamonds Farnsworth thought he could taste the fear he had left on this very spot two days earlier when, instead of going into the Blue Hole of Reina . . .

He had come up from its very soul!

48

THE BLACKNESS OF INNER SPACE VANISHED BENEATH the beams of light sweeping from the noses of Farallon DPVs and lanterns mounted in the hardshell helmets worn by the UDT divers.

Trailing behind the diver population vehicles, whose motors were off to conserve battery power, the divers glided into the myriad of colors reflecting from the coral wall.

Each man wore an RB-1 closed-circuit diving unit; consumed oxygen would circulate through a "scrubber" that would filter out the carbon dioxide, then return the unused oxygen to the tank, giving the divers an extended bottom time without the betrayal of exhausted bubbles, which could mark their location at the surface.

CPO Farnsworth floated down at his son's side; through the heavy plate of his face mask, he saw the blackness of the hole below. Occasionally he would punch the inflator on his buoyancy compensator, equalizing his buoyancy while slowing his descent to a smooth glide.

Checking his compass, Diamonds pointed east, then kicked hard, cutting his fins through the warm water.

Four minutes after submerging, the divers began to see the bottom come into view.

At 150 feet, the sandy surface was only a few feet away.

A steady hum droned in their ears as the first traces of nitrogen narcosis, "the rapture of the deep," began to narcotize their senses. Gliding onto the bottom, the men felt a warm, surging rush pulsating through their bodies.

"I feel like I've just drunk a pint of scotch," Diamonds said to Lovgren.

Lovgren giggled. "Yeah. Like a hard night out on the town. All we need is a couple of mermaids."

Through the short-range communications system worn by the divers, Daniel heard his father clearly from eight feet away.

If you gentlemen want to bullshit, do it while you work," Daniel ordered.

"How wide is this hole?" Lovgren asked.

"About a half mile. Give or take a few hundred yards," Diamonds replied.

Daniel quickly calculated the radius from the center. "Four hundred and forty yards. We have eight divers. Roughly one hundred and fifty feet per man."

"We best get to it, Diamonds," Lovgren said, motioning to the other divers in the team.

"We've got good visibility," said Diamonds. He swung his head out toward the blackness toward the wall. "I figure about fifty feet with the lights on the DPVs."

"What direction were you traveling when you went down?" asked Daniel.

Diamonds thought for a moment. "We were traveling east when we landed." Pointing to the eastern half of the hole, Diamonds suggested, "Let's start from the one-hundred-eighty-degree point, swinging around to zero degrees. That'll sweep out the entire eastern half."

Daniel agreed. "Chief Lovgren, I'll lead the sweep. You post in the middle as the pivot. Pop, you be the swing man on the end. If the satellite is correct, we should be close."

Lovgren lowered his DPV to the sandy bottom. CPO Farnsworth saw one of the UDT divers approach, carrying a large canvas bag. A red carabiner was attached to a rope at one end of the bag. A blue-painted carabiner was connected to a rope at the opposite end.

Diamonds connected the blue carabiner to his harness, then turned and began moving outbound behind the steady hum of his Farallon DPV.

At fifty-foot intervals, a red flag was tied to the rope. This would give the divers a reference mark to recognize the grid they were to search.

Reaching the wall, Diamonds reported to Daniel. "Swing man in place."

"Move out, Pop," Daniel ordered.

The long, slow sweep began with each diver traversing through his designated length of rope, scouring the bottom for the Hornet.

Fifteen minutes later, when the full eastern half had been swept, Chief Farnsworth sat at the zero degree magnetic point of the wall.

A chill threaded along his spine; not from the cold, since the water was warm. Rather, from what he had not heard.

"Did anybody find that fucking bird?" Farnsworth asked.

A long silence followed over the communications net.

Finally, Daniel's voice said what they already feared.

"The aircraft is gone!"

49

"WHAT DID YOU SAY? REPEAT THE LAST TRANSMISsion." Admiral Lord looked as though he was ready to eat the microphone connecting the *Valiant* to the *Gulf Raider*.

Cartography analyst Milton Floren sat staring incredulously at the satellite transmission receiving in infrared on the screen. *LaCrosse* was picking up heat emissions from nine bodies at the bottom of the hole.

The outline of the airplane was missing.

The events of the past two days had superceded continual monitoring of the blue hole; that, and the security problem maintaining the satellite directly over the site of the crash. Constant surveillance might have given the Cubans, or Russians, too many clues.

Never in his wildest nightmare had Lord thought the aircraft would be discovered.

"It couldn't have been recovered, sir," Floren insisted. "The Cubes would have been on surface radar. There's been no activity over the hole. None whatsoever."

Admiral Lord thought for a moment. Switching frequencies, he spoke quickly to the last man to see the Hornet.

"Wolf One . . . Home Plate. Are you monitoring the activity from station Tango?"

"Affirmative," Sacrette replied.

Flying in a long, oval pattern extending from Grand Cayman to Yucatán, Sacrette couldn't believe his ears.

"It could have been buried by the sand." Sacrette recalled Cucho telling him that the missing sphere had been buried by the storm surge.

"Negative," Lord replied. "They swept the area with metal detectors."

"Maybe it is in the west end of the hole."

"Negative. They've swept the entire hole. They found nothing, except an old Volkswagen that must have been dumped in the sea, then drifted along the bottom until it fell into the hole."

Admiral Lord stared at the infrared projection as he spoke.

"It sure as hell didn't fly out of there," Sacrette said.

Sacrette's comment reverberated inside Admiral Lord's head.

Fly!

Suddenly he leaned into the screen.

Pressing the microphone, he breathed heavily, "My God!"

50

SITTING ON THE BOTTOM OF THE BLUE HOLE, CPO Diamonds Farnsworth couldn't believe the order he heard coming over the commo net from Cody McKuen.

"You heard what the admiral ordered," Daniel said to his men. "Fan out and start looking."

The UDT divers charged toward the eastern wall behind the blue, filtered lights of the DPVs. Reaching the wall, the men spread out and, turning on their headlamps, which were also filtered with subdued blue to prevent surface detection, began searching the rocky wall of the blue hole.

Daniel skimmed along the bottom, looking, but saw nothing except the craggy base where the sand met the wall. Huge mounds of sand were piled against the wall where the storm surge had reshaped the bottom of the hole into an eerie underwater desert of dunes.

"Team, check in," Daniel ordered into his microphone.

"Not a fiddler's fuck," said Lovgren.

"Negative," Diamonds said.

The others reported negative results. Daniel glided

up a tall drift. As he pressed the button to communicate with the surface, he saw a quick, darting motion from the side.

Sharp, stinging pain streaked along his arm. "Damn! I need some help!"

Diamonds heard his son scream. Turning, he kicked furiously toward where Daniel was searching.

As he spotted Daniel, Diamonds's eyes widened. "Jesus Christ," he shouted, reaching for the sharp knife on his leg.

Daniel sat at the top of the mound, shaking his arm, which Diamonds could see had taken on a peculiar shape.

A shape made peculiar by the giant moray eel clutching Daniel's arm with razor-sharp teeth.

"You bastard! Let go of my baby!" Diamonds shouted as he raced up the tall dune.

With lightning speed, Diamonds's hand reached for the eel's head; the creature's eyes turned blue as the helmet light glowed off the two menacing orbs.

"The head," Daniel yelled. "The head!"

As Diamonds's knife blade found the eel's head, Diamonds saw his son disappear backward, where the peak of the sand dune caved away.

Diamonds head his grip!

Tumbling down the backside, the two men were momentarily lost in a cloud of swirling sand.

Searching frantically, Diamonds saw the eel's head jerk in and out of the blue flash from his headlamp.

Diamonds's arm raised, then thrust with all its strength.

"You bastard!"

The blade caught the eel; the head severed cleanly, disconnecting the two falling divers.

End over end they tumbled, until finally they slammed hard against what Diamonds thought was coral.

A loud, metallic ring echoed through the water.

Diamonds lay motionless for a moment; then, when he caught his breath, turned on his side.

Daniel was lying to his right; his arm was bleeding, sending a trail of blood into the water that turned blue under the light of Diamonds's lamp.

Diamonds looked at the arm. A queer expression spread across his face.

Noticing the look, Daniel mumbled, "I'm alright, Pop. You look like you just saw a ghost."

Diamonds nodded. The headlamp danced through the water, off the walls, then back.

Diamonds didn't notice the walls, or the fact that they were in a towering cave. He didn't notice that he was sitting on metal, rather than coral.

He didn't even notice the blood flowing from his son's arm.

"I'll be a son of a bitch!" Diamonds breathed. His hand was extended, pointing past Daniel.

Daniel turned to the side. He nearly choked. "Is that what I think it is, Pop?"

"It sure as hell is, son," Diamonds replied.

His hand was still raised, his finger pointing.

At the destructive weapon locked onto the starboard pylon of the wing the two divers were sitting on.

Gripping Daniel's bleeding arm, Diamonds laughed. "That's the baddest kid on the block . . . an AIM 9L Sidewinder missile!"

2330.

JOAQUIN ZARANTE ENTERED THE GULF OF GUACAN-ayabo from the southeast, hugging the Cuban coastline. In the cockpit he checked his position on the digital display and, satisfied that he was on course, spoke into the microphone.

"This is Joaquin Zarante. I will arrive in ten minutes. Have the patrol craft meet me as planned." He paused, then looked at the briefcase lying on the seat beneath the Stinger rocket he had perched on the floorboard.

Taking a pair of night glasses, he scanned the coastline. The rugged outline of French Soldier's Point burned green in the starlight field.

It was then that his suspicions were confirmed. An evil grin filled his face.

He saw what he had expected to find when he learned Dorffman was missing.

"So, my pretty. You are waiting. But I didn't expect you to be so foolish as to come this close to shore."

52

TWENTY MILES AWAY, HIDDEN IN THE DARK SHADOWS of the cove beneath French Soldier's Point, Cody McKuen turned to Conyers and Travers, who stood beside Lt. Commander Quinton Turk in the weak magenta light.

The *Gulf Raider* had slipped into the cove after inserting the UDT, and was now waiting to begin the next phase of the operation.

Removing the F/A-18 Hornet from the blackness of the Blue Hole of Reina.

But first there was the matter of Zarante. Who was now heading toward the opposite side of the cove. Toward the pier at the burned-out village of Santa Rosa.

Only he wasn't arriving as anticipated.

"Holy Christ!" exclaimed Cody. "If this is your package, Mr. Conyers, he's flying. But not in a seaplane."

Conyers looked at the weapons officer incredulously. "What do you mean?"

Cody was plotting the speed of the approaching blip. A blip that was not in the air.

A blip that was on the surface of the gulf.

Conyers raised a pair of starlight binoculars to his

eyes. In the distance he saw a low-profile speed boat approaching beneath a towering rooster tail of water.

"God damn." Conyers gave the glasses to Travers. "He's in a 'thunderboat.'"

Zarante was streaking toward the coast at over one hundred miles an hour in a one-thousand-horsepower "monster boat." The fastest sport racing boat in the world.

"Which means you can't sneak aboard the plane and grab him when he comes off the island," Lt. Commander Quinton Turk said flatly.

Conyers shook his head. He wore a look of defeat. "No. We'll have to scrap that idea." Looking at Travers, Conyers asked, "Any suggestions?"

Travers's eyebrows raised. "We could try to stop him on the way out."

Before he could say anything else, Cody interrupted.

"They've found the Hornet. It was in a cave. The current must have pushed the plane into the cave. The storm surge sealed off the cave with a wall of sand."

Skipper released a sigh of relief. "How long before they're ready to begin the extract?"

Cody fired the question to Lt. Daniel Farnsworth. Hearing his response, she replied, "They'll have to dig a channel through the sand. Lt. Farnsworth said the sand is soft. It shouldn't take more than thirty minutes."

Turk looked at Conyers. "Sorry, gentlemen. We've got nine men in that hole down there. And a classified aircraft. Not to mention 'Deep Throat' lying offshore. Any contact inside these waters could spell disaster. You'll have to wait for another time."

Raising the glasses, Conyers saw the boat disappear

around the other side of French Soldier's Point. Checking his watch, he saw that there might still be hope of getting the elusive Zarante.

"We'll continue with your mission. If we get lucky, we might get another shot at taking him alive. I trust you can outrun him in this boat, Commander Turk?"

Turk shrugged. "It depends on the lead he has. And where he's going."

Conyers's mouth tightened. "Then we'll wait. But one thing is for certain . . . he's not going to get away with those chemicals."

53

0000.

Zarante hurried through the main entrance of the concrete block production plant. Two officers greeted him; new faces, but the same Castro look-alike beards. The same wrinkled fatigues.

"Do you have the chemicals?" Zarante asked the first officer, a heavyset major.

"*Sí.* Do you have the payment?" He hoisted a heavy metal suitcase onto the table. Snapping the locks open, he lifted the lid, revealing four large metal containers.

Zarante grinned, then hoisted his briefcase onto the table. Opening the case with a flair, he stepped back, allowing the officers to look at the content.

"My God. What a beautiful sight."

Zarante took the container and, followed by the officers, returned to the jeep. Fifteen minutes later Zarante was delivered to the small pier at Santa Rosa. Slipping on his leather racing suit, he reached into the sophisticated cockpit and took out his helmet.

As he slipped the helmet on, he nonchalantly asked the heavyset officer, "Do you have any patrol boats in the area?"

The officer shook his head.

Zarante nodded knowingly. "I suggest you inspect the cove near French Soldier's Point. I saw a very unusual-looking vessel sitting in there. It appeared to be a hydroplane. An American hydroplane."

The officers looked at each other. The heavyset major shrugged. "A smuggler whose boat has broken down. We will find him. Take his drugs and boat. Then throw him in prison. It happens all the time."

Zarante laughed. "Tell me, Major. Do these drug smugglers carry a helicopter on the rear deck? Do they have missile pods on the bow?"

The major's face turned white. Rage followed. "Why didn't you tell me earlier?" He started for a pistol in his holster.

Zarante's hand came up lightning fast. He was holding a gun on the major. "I thought the boat was Cuban."

Motioning to the water, he ordered the major. "Throw the weapon in the water. Then get your fat Cuban ass out of here. Our business is finished. If the Americans are here to catch me, it's because of you blundering fools."

The soldiers complied. Zarante climbed into the tight-fitting cockpit and fired the four 250-horsepower overhead cam engines.

Seconds later he screamed along the surface, riding on the leading edge of a towering rooster tail of water.

He wasn't worried about the American boat. He knew they would soon have their hands full.

54

CPO DIAMONDS FARNSWORTH SAT IN THE COCKPIT OF the night-configured Hornet; Lt. Farnsworth was on his knees beneath the nose gear. Daniel watched Lovgren attach a cable around the gear strut.

"That's got her, sir. She's clamped tighter than a yard dog's jawbone," Lovgren said, looking toward the darkness.

In the subdued blue light, a thick cable rose upward, disappearing in the darkness overhead, where the blue light ended abruptly.

Switching to the communication channel connecting him to the *Raider*, Daniel reported to Lt. Commander Turk. "Ready for extract, sir."

Standing at the controls, Quint eased the throttles forward, propelling the Hornet along the course programmed into the navigation computer. The exact reverse of the course the *Raider* took to weave through the mine field guarding the mouth of the Gulf of Guacanayabo.

"Hang on, Lt. Farnsworth. We're getting under way. Taking up the slack," Turk told Daniel.

A long cable ran from a winch positioned on the rear

deck of the *Raider*, and ran over the side, where it disappeared into the water.

In the Hornet's cockpit, Diamonds felt the slack from the cable apply tension as he reached for the HOTAS. Quickly he wiped out the cockpit by moving the stick right, then left, checking the ailerons for deflection. They were stiff but workable; he glanced to the starboard wing and saw sand slip off the wing where the aileron moved.

Pressing the rudder pedals, he turned to the tail section and saw the rudders move.

"We've got an airplane, sir," Diamonds said to Daniel. "You best get your boys hooked up."

The eight UDT men took long static lines from pouches attached to the DPVs. Within seconds they had hooked the static lines to one of the nine hardpoints on the underside of the Hornet, fired up the motors, and moved forward of the sleek needle-nose.

Joined by a cable from the surface, and with the added tow from the DPVs, the Hornet was ready to make her final flight.

"We've got movement," said Diamonds.

The cable tightened like the shaft of an arrow. Slowly, then more quickly, the fighter rolled forward.

The water churned as the DPVs were maxed out; the winch on the *Raider* began winding faster . . . faster.

On the surface, the *Raider* increased speed to thirty knots.

The Hornet rolled along the sandy bottom and, as Diamonds hauled gently back on the HOTAS, rose from the floor of the Blue Hole of Reina.

"We're airborne. Or seaborne. Or whatever the hell we are . . . we are," Diamonds reported to Turk.

Applause broke out in the pilothouse of the *Raider*.

"I had my doubts," said Daniel, who was talking from his position in front of the nose. "I didn't think this airplane could glide underwater."

"Simple principles of flight and aerodynamics. Lift over drag. Thrust over weight. With the aircraft in the water, the weight is nearly at neutral buoyancy from the water density. Now, let's see if we can get some lift and get the hell out of here."

Hauling back on the HOTAS, Diamonds raised the angle of attack to twenty degrees of pitch.

"Yeah," Lovgren shouted, watching the Hornet rise upward. "Yeah!"

The computerized winch kept pace by tightening the slack through its electronic sensitivity load calculator.

The giant fighter rose gloriously from its watery grave.

"We're almost there," Diamonds said, checking his depth gauge. The gauge read forty feet.

At the thirty-foot mark, the lip of the blue hole appeared. The sudden change of current forced Diamonds to apply right rudder to offset the drift.

In the pilothouse, Quinton wore a broad grin. "I'll be damned. It's working." He knew the fighter was now at thirty feet beneath the surface, where it would remain until the next phase of the mission.

"Let's get the hell out of Cuba," Turk ordered. "We've got to rendezvous with 'Deep Throat.'"

At her console, Cody started to say something, when—suddenly—her eyes widened on the screen.

"Oh, God!" she said loudly, looking at the radar screen.

Four blips suddenly burned against the soft green field.

55

In the *Valiant*'s CIC, Admiral Lord stiffened as he saw four blips appear on the radar screen.

"We've got bandits coming off the deck, Admiral," the technician said, plotting the course of the Cuban fighters. "They're flying an intercept toward Tango station."

Lord took the microphone and spoke quickly to the TAC CAP. "Wolf Two . . . deploy to station Tango. Provide tactical canopy. Observe ROE. Do not fire on the Cubans unless fired upon. Repeat. Do not fire on Cubans unless hostile intent is shown."

"Roger, Home Plate. Wolf Pack," Domino's voice replied over the CIC's intercom. A split second later the men in the combat information center heard Domino issue the order to assume attack formation.

"Fangs out!" Domino ordered the fighter pilot's battle cry, meaning when the fighter pilot goes to attack maneuvering, he knows the biting fangs of the gravity viper will come out.

In the sky above Puerto Rico the VFA-101 squadron went to full Zone Five afterburner thrust.

In the sky over Grand Cayman, where he was stationed to track the elusive Zarante, Sacrette was listening on the communications system. Looking out the cockpit, he could see the tail section of a Grumman KA-6D Intruder. A long fuel line extended from the former strike airplane converted to tanker. At the end of the line, a round "basket" was connected to Sacrette's starboard refueling probe.

"Spitting the basket," Sacrette called to the pilot of the Intruder. Sacrette disconnected the refueling, kicked right rudder, and rolled to the inverted.

On the HOTAS, Sacrette went to Zone Five. Instantly the Hornet shot from transonic to supersonic.

The sky above Cayman Brac shook as the Thunderbolt aimed the nose of his fighter toward a chain of islands he would recognize in his sleep.

The Jardines de la Reina.

56

"TALLY HO!" DOMINO BARKED TO THE FOUR STRIKE/ Fighters flying in wing formation off his three and nine o'clock positions.

On the HUD, the FLIR was displaying four MiG-25 Foxbats approaching an intercept point above the *Gulf Raider*, which Domino couldn't see without "slewing" the FLIR to his port, costing him valuable time and, more important, the positioning requirement.

"Let's mix it up," Domino ordered. "Wolf Three . . . and Four. Take the two on the starboard. Wolf Five . . . and Six. Take the two to port."

From the right and left, four F/A-18 Hornets rolled to the inverted, diving for the deck.

Domino's mind flashed the age-old rules of air combat that still applied today, though first outlined by the German aviator Oswald Boelke in World War I:

> Secure all possible advantage before attacking.
> If you initiate an attack, carry it through.
> Fire only at close range.
> Keep your eye on your opponent.

Attack your opponent from behind.

If an opponent dives to attack you, turn and meet him.

Remember your line of retreat.

Fly and fight in groups of four or six; if you break into single combat, don't have several aircraft attacking the same opponent.

But this was night, and there were no solid rules for night fighting. Except the most important one: Get the opponent before they get you.

The Hornet streaked for the surface, then shot straight up into a hammerhead, surrounding the MiGs.

Realizing they were in a knife fight, the Cuban pilots broke formation, twisting and turning through the sky as the Fighting Hornets of VFA-101 tried to divert the MiGs away from the *Gulf Raider*.

It was then that Domino cursed his luck, "Damn. I've got no joy. No joy. I've lost them. Keep your eyes open." The exec alerted the others that he had lost visual contact.

"No joy," reported Wolf Four.

Domino gripped the HOTAS; how he wished the fighters were night-configured.

"Slew the FLIR," Domino ordered.

Crazily, the fighters began twisting through the sky, covering large amounts of area in order to use the FLIR cameras to hunt for the MiGs.

It was like the proverbial search for a needle in a haystack.

"I got joy!" shouted Wolf Five.

Lt. Tinker Jellico, running name Jelly, eyeballed the HUD. A MiG Foxbat was coming out of a steep, turning dive. Straight for his twelve.

"He's coming on my twelve. Request permission to fire."

"Negative," Domino replied, hating to leave his man sitting on the edge, waiting for the MiG to open fire first.

In his cockpit, Jelly shook his head. "The hell you say."

Jelly maneuvered the "tipper" on the heads-up display until the descending Foxbat was in the box.

"Lock him up," Jelly ordered the RIO.

"What?" the RIO replied.

"Lock his ass up. I'm not going to let some goddamn Cuban decide if we live or die!"

From the pit, there was a sigh, then the RIO "locked up" the MiG-25 with his APG-65 radar weapons system.

The puck was on the ice.

"Do you want to play . . . or practice?" Jelly asked the image.

The Cuban in the MiG would be hearing the howling shrill indicating his heat source had been sensed, and his bird was locked up to the Hornet's weapons system.

Decision time.

"Come on, baby. Make my day," Jelly shouted. "Make my day." He couldn't fire until the MiG broke the rules, which he knew he had already done by initiating lock-on to the MiG.

But what the hell, he told himself. *A broken rule is better than losing the advantage.*

As though he could hear, the MiG pilot responded with a vertical afterburner climb, trying to shake the Hornet.

Jelly was on his tail, kicking rudders, working the

HOTAS like a frenzied piccolo player.

They shot through Angels eighteen, where the MiG rolled to inverted, then dove again at the Hornet.

"That tears it. He's got his radar on us," shouted Lt. Bob "Rooster" Brewster, the RIO.

Jellico grinned. "You want to play."

Jelly pressed the red firing switch, then reported into the boom mike, indicating the launch of a Sidewinder missile. "Fox Two."

The heat-seeking missile streaked through the sky. Closeness to the target eliminated most of the Cuban's evasive maneuvering. Tiny fireballs of flares lit the sky in a long necklace of light as the Cuban pilot tried to lure the Sidewinder to the heat of the flares.

"Too late, baby." Jelly laughed. On the HUD, the heat signature of the MiG was dancing through the night; the Sidewinder turned with each move.

In the next instant the blackness above the Caribbean radiated as a red-orange explosion turned night into momentary day.

"Yeah!" shouted Jelly. "Yeah!"

It was his first kill

The celebration was short-lived as the cry of Domino's voice broke the commo net.

"He's on me. He's on me!"

Jelly looked out the cockpit.

Nothing. He could see nothing except the lights of the Cuban coast.

Domino knew he couldn't outrun the MiG, which the Cuban pilot would know as well. Figuring the Cuban had never flown against a Hornet, Domino utilized the feature that made the Hornet the toughest fighter in the sky, even against faster aircraft.

The turn rate.

In aerial combat, turn rate is more important than speed. Turning brings you onto an enemy. Turn rate can switch the tables, turning the pursued into the pursuer.

Hauling left on the HOTAS, Domino banked ninety degrees and hauled back on the pole.

The Hornet banked into a 180-degree "bat-turn," so named for the same turn the Batmobile executed in the old television series *Batman*.

The force of nine g's instantly inflated Domino's speed jeans and pushed his head deep into his helmet. Thought and vision narrowed, as though he were looking through a telescope from the opposite end.

Rolling out, Domino saw the fiery tail of the MiG above his two o'clock.

"Gotcha," said Domino as he pressed the firing switch on his M-61 20mm cannon.

A steam of red uranium-tipped, armored-piercing bullets the size of flashlight batteries spit from the gunport above the radome nose cone.

In seconds the radar was directing the bullets into the heat source with deadly effect.

The MiG disintegrated two hundred yards from Domino's nose, forcing the pilot to pitch immediately to full vertical afterburner climb to avoid the exploding MiG's flaming debris.

Then a chilling sound came over the commo net.

"I'm locked. I'm locked. No joy. No joy." Wolf Six's voice was tinged with fear at hearing the shrill of lock-on from a pursuing MiG.

Suddenly a voice broke. Calm. Familiar.

"Wolf Six, take the MiG to vertical. I've got him off my six. Stand by."

Captain Boulton Sacrette had given an order. Looking through his "Cat's Eyes" goggles, the night-configured CAG could see the swept wing outline of the Foxbat chasing the young American fighter pilot.

"Now," Sacrette called. "Hit the deck!"

Watching the Hornet suddenly roll over, Sacrette had a clear field of fire at the MiG, which was now reaching the top, pulling into inverted.

Sacrette, too, chose the nose gun. It was the only way for a real fighter pilot to fight.

Taking him from his nine, Sacrette sighted the MiG's cockpit, then pressed the wind-correcting cannon's trigger.

Instantly the MiG was joined to the Hornet by a river of furious molten-steel projectiles. Through the blue-green field, Sacrette saw the MiG's cockpit suddenly disappear; the pilot's head seemed to be missing as well.

The MiG rolled left, then fell from the sky, its left wing separated at the fuselage.

"That's for Blade. And Axeman. You son of a bitch!"

57

"THREE DOWN, AND THE LAST ONE LEFT IS TURNING tail, Skipper!" Cody McKuen shouted over the excitement in the pilothouse.

On the radar screen, a single blip was turning back toward Cuba. The five blips of the Wolf Pack formed a tight formation over the *Gulf Raider*, giving them a tactical air cover should the Cubans come back to fight.

"I think they've had enough," said Skipper Turk, grinning at the radar.

Taking the mike, Turk called Sacrette, "Well done, Wolf Pack. Keep the area clear. We're scheduled to rendezvous with 'Deep Throat' in ten minutes."

But not everyone in the pilothouse was as happy as Turk. Travers took the mike. "Wolf One . . . this is Travers. Our package is heading south. Toward Haiti. Request you intercept."

"Roger," Sacrette replied.

On the radar screen, the blip of Sacrette's Hornet was turning south, toward Haiti, in pursuit of another blip being tracked by satellite.

The blip of Joaquin Zarante.

Turk looked at Travers. The soldier was watching

the drug smuggler's radar signature. Then a smile crawled across his face as he saw Sacrette's blip closing on Zarante.

"We're home free," Travers said.

Turk shook his head. "Not quite. We've still got a plane to recover. I only hope the UDT team is still in one piece."

Thirty feet below the *Raider's* planform, CPO Diamonds Farnsworth knew nothing about the brief air battle. He was having his own battle while flying the Hornet through a water-filled sky.

The DPVs were now below the wings, providing a trailing, stabilizing tension as the fighter was being towed out to sea at more than thirty knots.

Traveling exposed at thirty knots beneath the surface was not the same as traveling thirty knots on the surface. The density of the rushing water nearly ripped the HOTAS from Diamonds's hands; his head was bent as the powerful, steady wall of water pulled at his helmet.

His muscles ached; his hands cramped around the HOTAS. Pressing the rudder, he felt like he was trying to push a building over onto its side.

The pressure seemed endless. Sweat poured from his forehead, burning the sensitive tissue in his eyes.

"I'm about to give out," Diamonds moaned into the microphone.

From his position beneath the fighter, Daniel heard his father's strained voice. "Hang on, Pop. We're almost there."

"Don't . . . know . . . if . . . I . . . can . . ." the strained voice of the CPO replied.

Daniel thought for a moment. "When I was a kid, you told me pain is all in your mind. That you can overcome pain by forgetting it. Forget the pain. Pick out an object on the horizon and concentrate on that point."

Diamonds looked to the front. Through the plowing water coming off the nose he saw nothing except the blackness beyond where his blue light ended.

Daniel tried to look up, the steady impact of the water nearly snapping his neck as his head moved.

Below, the bottom was rapidly falling off.

"We're getting close," he shouted to his father. "Hang on."

The minutes passed like hours; yet the UDT men hung to their DPVs. Diamonds gripped the HOTAS while holding the nose in an even, steady glide path.

Sirens started screaming in Diamonds's ears; he thought he saw a black-skinned mermaid swim by as the shrill turned to a thunder.

The noise grew; pounding the water.

His fingers started to slip; his body, buckled into the front seat, ached where the straps were cutting through his wetsuit.

Still the thunder grew, both in intensity and in closeness.

Shielding the front of the face plate, he looked through the plowing water folding back from the nose.

In the distance something gray appeared, then began to turn black.

"'Deep Throat,'" Diamonds whispered gratefully.

In that instant, the plowing water settled; the thunder turned to a soft hum.

Twenty yards away external running lights could be seen. Black-clad figures swam toward the Hornet, framed in the light beaming from the "Deep Throat."

The code name for the battle group's nuclear submarine, USS *Defender*.

58

JOAQUIN ZARANTE SMILED AT HIS GOOD FORTUNE. The lights of Port-au-Prince were visible in the distance. Friends were there. Paid-for friends. Not to be trusted except through money, the greatest ally-forming bond in the world.

Music was playing from the tapedeck; outside, he could see the stars.

The steady purr of the four "monster boat" engines gave the music a soft, soothing backdrop.

Night on the sea. Stars in the sky. Moon over Port-au-Prince.

And the metal suitcase lying beneath the Stinger rocket. He was drunk with power.

Reaching to adjust the mixture of one engine, he suddenly stiffened as another sound interfered with the music and drone of his engines.

Suddenly—the windshield exploded!

The thunder of a jet ripped the surface into a geysering storm of rising columns of water.

Glass flew, slicing his leather suit; his knuckles stung where the Plexiglas shards had been pulverized into flying shards that stitched his hands with needlelike holes.

"Bastard!" Zarante shouted as his eyes narrowed on the fiery red tail of an airplane pulling into a vertical dive fifty yards in front of his thunderboat.

In the cockpit of his Hornet, another form of thunder was preparing to greet Zarante with another bolt of lightning.

A thunderbolt.

Sacrette eased the throttle back to military power from Zone Five, banked hard right, and turned an eight-g bat-turn.

Lining up on the thunderboat, Sacrette gripped the HOTAS. At the precise moment the thunderboat appeared on his twelve, Sacrette went to Zone Five afterburner and hauled back on the pole.

Ten feet above the surface, a red tail of raw burning fuel spread a twenty-foot-wide carpet of hellacious fury.

Zarante's eyes widened as he saw the water exploding toward him from one hundred feet away.

Enveloped in the spewing geysers, the thunderboat rose into the air, held there momentarily by the surging energy of the water.

Then, nosing forward, the craft arced toward the sea, turning on its side just before it slammed through the surface.

In the cockpit Zarante cursed as it filled with water; he tried to scream again but water filled his lungs.

Sitting in a sea of green water, Zarante's eyes bulged as he looked to the right seat.

"No!" he screamed despite the water in his lungs. Bubbles shot from his mouth, toward the metallic suitcase, which was pitching forward from the seat of the plummeting craft.

His hand reached again, but fell inches short as the

case danced lightly through the hole where the glass was shattered.

The sensation of sinking stopped; the baffled flotation compartments of the boat reversed the downward plunge, then rode the craft back to the surface.

All thoughts of power were gone; the chemicals meant nothing to Zarante.

Revenge consumed his thoughts. His soul.

The sound of the fighter plane could be heard; glancing around, he saw the red tail of the Hornet as it was climbing into the sky.

"You motherfucker!" he breathed while reaching into the right seat, where the Stinger was wedged between the seat and firewall. "I will show you how we treat airplanes in the Huallaga."

Zarante raised the shoulder-fired missile; quickly he armed the device, sighted, and pulled the trigger.

The explosion clapped resoundingly across the surface, preceding the rocket that streaked toward the fighter plane approaching low on the horizon.

Sacrette's stomach tightened as the alarm system in his fighter began shrieking. A coldness spread through him.

Damn! He had been here before. In the Med, when he lost Munchy four months earlier from a similar attack launched by a crazed PLO terrorist.

Only there was a difference: then, he was at minimal controllable airspeed.

Now . . . he was at Zone Five afterburner!

Hauling back on the HOTAS, Sacrette went to pure vertical climb; the condensation trailing off his wing roots wafted backward, toward the supersonic missile.

He didn't have time to go to ECM; there was no

time for electronic countermeasures. There was only time to get to as many angels as possible.

Ten thousand.

Twelve thousand.

The shrill of the closing missile grew louder. Closer.

Fifteen thousand.

Now!

Sacrette's hand flashed to the instrument panel, and with a single move, he cut the power in both engines.

Silence would have been complete except for the eerie whisper outside the cockpit.

He banked hard right, pulled back on the HOTAS, and grinned at the approaching Stinger.

The missile streaked harmlessly past his clamshell cockpit, then disappeared into the sky.

"You need a lesson in shooting," Sacrette said acidly while reaching to the CPU on the panel.

He based his engine shutdown decision on one of the unique features of the Hornet. The CPU allows for starting the Hornet's engines without an external power source required by most aircraft.

With a flick of his wrist he set the power, threw the switch, and fired the port engine.

When he lit the starboard engine, he was back in business.

"How many more missiles do you have, Zarante?" Sacrette asked the silhouette of the thunderboat, which was coming up on his twelve. "I'll wager you have none."

His answer came in the flash of fire from the thunderboat.

Sacrette laughed. "You've got to be kidding." He switched to the M-61 20mm cannon.

"Okay, Zarante," he whispered. "We'll do it the

old-fashioned way. A hang-town shootout."

Joaquin Zarante stood in the cockpit of his thunderboat, firing his pistol at the approaching fighter plane.

It was futile, he knew; but it was all he had.

He saw a golden stream flash from the nose of the fighter; the bullets stitched a neat, two-sided path toward his boat.

Zarante's thoughts suddenly flashed to the Huallaga Valley. To the old ones of the Shining Path.

How he hated them for being so goddamned right!

The wall of steel found Zarante waiting.

In a shower of bullets, his arms disappeared.

His trunk was severed at the waist.

There was no pain, only the quick ending as the murderous vacuum pulled Joaquin Zarante into blackness.

59

"WOLF ONE . . . TO HOME PLATE. PACKAGE DELIV-ered." That was all Sacrette said. Before a reply could be heard, he turned off the communications system on the HOTAS.

Settling into his Martin-Baker ejection seat, Captain Boulton Sacrette removed the "Cat's Eyes" goggles. The sky was now black. The stars were twinkling beneath a clear sky.

He had made a decision. One he might regret. Nonetheless, a decision.

His blue eyes skipped to the horizon.

In the distance, lights could be seen faintly.

"What the hell," he said aloud. "Get it done."

The sky shook as the Hornet went to Zone Five.

Climbing to thirty thousand feet, Sacrette shut down all emitter systems. He was passive.

A night fighter. Slipping on the Cat's Eyes, he saw in the distance a finger of land jútting from the Cuban coast.

Reaching a point six miles directly above French Soldier's Point, Sacrette shoved the nose over, then banked left into a steep dive.

The attack dive.

The Hornet screamed past Mach one. The sky shook in his wake. At twenty thousand feet he turned on the weapons system.

His fingers played the piccololike HOTAS; deftly he made ready to use the weapon stored beneath his right wing.

At five thousand feet, Sacrette laser-scanned a dense jungle area. On the screen, he saw one part of the jungle emit a stronger laser backscatter from the additional barbed wire and metal filters mounted on the roof of the target he sought.

Smiling, he released the two-thousand-pound laser-guided bomb from his Hornet. On the HUD, he saw the bomb angling on a path for its target, a square, concrete block building now locked up beneath the jungle canopy.

He didn't need to see the building. He knew it was there. Guiding the bomb, he watched it disappear through the jungle canopy.

A quaking, tremendous explosion followed as the bomb struck the building that produced the horrible killer germs.

In a thunderous blast that reached thousands of feet into the air, La Casa del Diablo disappeared from the face of the earth.

60

0100.

CAPTAIN BOULTON SACRETTE'S CONCENTRATION WAS glued to the fresnel lens on the port side of the USS *Valiant*. The fresnel, or the "ball" as it's known, gives the pilots a visual reference of horizontal lights to use as a visual slope approach indicator in achieving the most difficult task in flying: an arrested landing aboard an elevated deck moving through the ocean.

Lining up his aircraft, he pressed the landing gear button; momentarily, he felt the nitrogen charge fire the Hornet's landing gear into the down and locked position.

"Call the ball. Thunderbolt," came the voice of the air boss from the carrier.

"Hornet ball. Three point four." After he gave his aircraft type, the fresnel would be adjusted to the specific angle required to bring the Hornet onto the deck at the right glide angle. Three point four meant he had a little over three hundred pounds of remaining fuel.

As he crossed the threshold at 140 miles an hour, Sacrette's Hornet slammed the deck, hitting wire three dead-solid-perfect. In the next instant he did what might appear insane: He went to full military power.

This is done in the event that the cable doesn't hold,

or the cable is missed. In which case, the plane is under power and ready to begin a takeoff run, instead of rolling off the deck into the sea.

The cable held. Sacrette taxied off the runway.

The deck was filled with thousands of shouting, hooraying men.

One young woman.

And one small boy.

Cucho Clemente walked beside Diamonds Farnsworth, who appeared tired, but smiling. Daniel walked at his side.

As the CAG climbed down from his cockpit, he was greeted by the excited pilots and crew, all of whom had taken part in recovering the Hornet, stopping Zarante, and kicking the Cubans' asses.

Lt. Commander Quinton Turk stood with his crew, Tillis and Cody; their eyes were shining with the knowledge that they had passed the test of combat.

The UDT divers were behind Daniel; around them gathered a large crowd.

"Where's my Hornet?" Sacrette asked Farnsworth.

Diamonds jerked his finger to the rear of the carrier. "We're off-loading her from the sub. She's ruined, of course. But she's here. Safe. And still top secret."

Sacrette shook hands with the men, and Cody. Raising Cucho in his arms, he saw the pride flashing in the boy's eyes.

"When do we go to Montana, Thunderbolt?" Cucho asked.

"Soon," he said softly. Looking at the crowd, he saw the throng begin to part in the middle.

Admiral Elrod Lord approached, wearing a grim mask.

"Maybe sooner than you think, Cucho," Sacrette said.

It was now time to pay the fiddler.

Lord stopped and leaned into Sacrette's face. "It's my understanding you took it upon yourself to bomb that Cuban facility, despite my direct orders to the contrary. Is that correct?"

Sacrette nodded. "I felt the facility needed to be bombed. Yes, sir. I dropped one bomb. The facility is gone."

Some sporadic applause broke out, which Lord silenced with a sweeping glare.

"I have a problem, Captain Sacrette." Lord said 'Captain' as though it might not be appropriate any longer.

"What's that, sir?"

"Whether to court-martial you . . . or recommend you for a decoration." Lord was now grinning.

Sacrette looked confused. "I don't understand," he said cautiously.

"Apparently, the president shares your feelings about destroying the chemical plant. His authorization arrived several minutes before you made your bomb run. Which, I'm glad to say, pulls you out of the deep blue sea."

Lord extended his hand.

As they shook hands, the applause exploded. Sacrette grinned. "The president's a good man. I knew he'd come around to my way of thinking."

61

CHIEF DIAMONDS FARNSWORTH SLIPPED OUT OF THE shadows beneath the island. He wore the look of a man committing adultery for the first time.

Under his arm he carried two canvas bags; he carried the bags as though they contained the Holy Grail.

Stopping at a SH-60 Seahawk, Farnsworth leaned through the door and whispered conspiratorially. "Are you ready?"

Leaning to the door from the cockpit, Sacrette replied, "Let's get to it, Chief."

The chief slide into the right seat. Seconds later Sacrette started the engines. When the powerful turboshafts reached lift-off revolutions, Sacrette eased the helo into the air; seconds later the sleek helo disappeared over the edge of the flight deck.

Skimming ten feet above the surface, Sacrette turned on the moving map display. A chain of islands appeared. Picking the one he knew was his target, he banked east by northeast.

Switching the turboprops to the "whisper" mode, Sacrette sat back in the seat. Neither men said a word.

This was not the moment for talk.

It was the moment of contemplation.

On through the night the machine charged, until the Seahawk reached the island on the map display.

Remembering the cove on Cayo Grande, Sacrette eased the helo onto the beach where he witnessed the crash of one of his squadron's Hornets.

The Hornet was gone.

He prayed that nothing else had been disturbed.

Moving quickly, they made their way to the clearing in the jungle. Tracks covered the soft sand, making Sacrette's pulse quicken.

"Did they find them?" Diamonds asked hesitantly.

"Let's find out," Sacrette replied.

Using a small entrenching tool, Sacrette carefully scraped at the soft sand covering his two pilots.

Farnsworth watched quietly, noting how Sacrette uncovered the bodies as thought the two men might still be alive. Or could be hurt by the blade.

Finally, Sacrette sat back on his knees.

The face of Lt. Darrel "Blade" Blaisedale could be seen from the sandy cocoon wrapping his body.

"Give me the flags." Sacrette reached over to Diamonds.

Diamonds opened the canvas containers; respectfully, he removed two red, white, and blue American flags. "You know, Thunderbolt. There's some people in America who say it's alright to burn this flag. They say it's a form of expressing their right of speech under the First Amendment."

Sacrette took the first flag and began wrapping it around Blade's body. "Yeah. And there's some people who die for the flag. Like these two fine young men.

That's also a form of speech."

Diamonds thought for a moment. "I like what Blade and Axeman are saying a helluva lot more than the flag burners."

Sacrette looked proudly at the face of Axeman. As he covered the youthful face, he said softly, "So do I, Chief."

Sacrette rose to attention. Farnsworth did the same, standing across from the CAG.

Between them lay the flag-covered bodies of their men. Their friends. Their countrymen.

Simultaneously, both men raised their right hand.

There, in the darkness of a Communist state, they held their salutes, long and proud.

"Come on, Chief Farnsworth," Sacrette said, bending down to Blade. "Let's take them home."

Minutes later the Seahawk lifted off the island; instead of turning west, toward the carrier, Sacrette flew north.

Toward the navy base on the southern tip of the Florida Keys.

To America.

The High Rockies. Montana.

A CRISP BREEZE WHIPPED THROUGH THE RUGGED Madison Range mountains, creating a low, moaning concerto from the rubbing branches of tall pine, the towering cottonwood and aspen blanketing the high Rockies overlooking the sprawling Madison Valley south of Bozeman.

To the south, Sphinx Peak rose in ancient splendor; to the east, in the valley, the rising sun was just touching Ennis Lake, giving the clear, clean water the shiny reflection of mirrored glass.

Against the thin darkness on the east bench of the range, three shadows moved slowly along a narrow, winding trail. Nearing a plateau, two of the shadows appeared taller than the third, which was thin and short.

Cucho Clemente, bundled against the chill, followed the taller man to his front; a man who had once been a stranger, but now was his savior.

Behind Cucho walked another man; similar in appearance to the one in front of Cucho, he, too, was tall.

He, too, had the rugged face that seemed to be carved from the very stone surrounding them.

They all wore down-filled waistcoats, Levi's, and western boots. On their heads they wore old cowboy hats;

except Cucho, whose hat was new.

Reaching the plateau, Captain Boulton Sacrette stopped, where he always had as a young boy. He turned, faced the east, then shouted his name toward the vast openness plummeting into the wide valley that seemed to stretch endlessly.

"Boulton Sacrette." The name echoed down the ridge, crashed against a deep cavern, then shot back into the air, repeating the name of the fighter pilot who once trapped and hunted the Madison Range.

"Try it, Cucho." Boulton motioned toward the valley.

"Cucho Clemente." His name spilled over the edge, reverberated, echoed back, then faded into the void below.

"What do you think, Dad?" Boulton turned to the tall man standing behind Cucho.

Adrian Sacrette was an older version of his son. Although his dark hair was now gray, the blue eyes were the same, burning with the same intensity. His voice was a proud voice; like the man.

Standing behind Cucho, Adrian's hands, which looked like twists of dried vine, rested on the boy's shoulders. Giving Cucho a gentle squeeze, the father replied, "I think he'll do. He reminds me of another little boy that used to climb these mountains."

Boulton led the way to where the trail ended against a solid wall of granite. Looking up, Cucho thought the wall rose into the heavens.

Boulton walked to where two boulders rested against each other. Heavy brush jutted from a crack between the ground and where the boulders met, but it was easily cleared by the fighter pilot.

The cleared-away crack measured about two feet wide, large enough for Boulton to slip through. Just before he disappeared, he said to Cucho, "Come on. I have something I want you to see."

Cucho looked at Adrian. A curious look was on the boy's face, but Adrian nodded gently, and trusting both men, Cucho followed.

Slipping through the crack, Cucho felt there was something familiar about the place, as though he might have been there before. But then, that was impossible. He told himself so in the deep, rich darkness.

It was then that a light came on.

Boulton was shining a flashlight.

"A dugout!" Cucho shouted.

Cucho stood at the mouth of a large cavern guarded by the giant boulders. On the walls were ancient paintings of funny-looking men with long hair riding horses and shooting arrows at what he had learned was an animal called the buffalo.

"It's an old Indian cave. I found it when I was about your age."

Shining the light to the rear of the cave, Boulton went to a ledge, where he picked up an old suitcase lying beneath years of undisturbed dust. A quick shake, and the dust flew.

Opening the suitcase, Boulton shined a light into the darkened container.

"Wow!" Cucho exclaimed. "They are beautiful."

Hundreds of Indian arrowheads, mallet heads, bits of arrow, and colorful beads filled the suitcase.

"I found this over there." Holding a spent rifle cartridge, he pointed to a corner of the cave. "I've never taken these things out of here. I felt like they belonged here. That they were a part of this place. Forever."

Before Cucho could say anything, Boulton remembered something important.

Reaching into his pocket, Boulton took out an object that made Cucho's eyes widen. And his heart ache with memory.

A round, shiny sphere the size of a baseball.

Looking at Adrian, Boulton told Cucho his reason for returning to Montana sooner than expected.

"My dad has told me about the dreams. About the nightmares."

Tears rolled down Cucho's cheeks. "I get so afraid."

Boulton took the boy in his arms; he realized it was the first time in his life he had comforted a crying child.

It was a good feeling. It was how his father had comforted him as a little boy.

"You've had a rough time. Rougher than any kid I've ever known. But it happened. There's no backing away. It's something you have to learn to forget."

"How?" Cucho asked, wiping at his tears.

Sacrette smiled, then touched the boy on the forehead. "I'm going to take all those bad dreams and put them in your ball."

He opened the ball, and flicked his fingers at the two opened holes. Closing the sphere that sealed the devil water from La Casa del Diablo, he dropped the ball-like container into the suitcase and closed the lid.

"The bad dreams are in there. They can't hurt you." Carrying the suitcase to the ledge, Boulton swung his arms up, placing the suitcase on the ledge.

Without a word, Boulton handed Cucho the flashlight and walked to the opening of the cave. Adrian followed.

Sitting alone, Cucho looked at the ledge, at the suitcase he knew was in darkness. Then he laughed like the little boy he was.

He flashed the light onto the suitcase. The pain seemed to fade.

Cucho Clemente walked to the crack in the wall. Peering through, he saw Boulton Sacrette framed against the shining light of morning.

A thought came to mind.

He thought of the names he had heard in the two weeks since he had come to live with Adrian Sacrette.

Jim Bridger. Jeremiah Johnson. Sitting Bull. Theodore Roosevelt.

Heroes. American heroes. Larger than life.

Cucho added a name to the list of heroes.

A fighter pilot from Montana.

Boulton Sacrette.

A former paratrooper and combat veteran of Viet Nam, Tom Willard holds a commercial pilot's license and has lived in Zimbabwe and the Middle East. He now lives in Grand Forks, North Dakota.